The Earth Weighs Heavy

ALSO BY ALISON JOSEPH

SISTER AGNES MYSTERIES
Book 1: Thou Shalt Not Kill
Book 2: Thou Shalt Not Bear False Witness
Book 3: Honour Thy Father
Book 4: False Idols
Book 5: A Hymn of Death
Book 6: Shadow of Death
Book 7: Cast the First Stone
Book 8: A Poisoned Chalice
Book 9: The Earth Weighs Heavy

A SISTER AGNES MYSTERY

THE EARTH *WEIGHS* HEAVY

ALISON JOSEPH

JOFFE BOOKS

Joffe Books, London
www.joffebooks.com

First published in Great Britain in 2025

Cover art by Dee Dee Book Covers

ISBN: 978-1-80573-322-5

PROLOGUE

It was the day that the flood came. An ordinary London day. Even the March sun shone, at times. But the clouds darkened and scudded in the jittery wind. In the streets, passers-by looked nervously towards the sky as they walked to work or ran for a bus, or pushed their child in its pram.

Afterwards, they would say, 'Who'd have thought? Who'd have thought we'd be running for cover as the deluge crashed around us, wind-blown torrents felling awnings, trees and roofs, overflowing drains, turning streets to rivers, escalators to cascades? Who'd have thought we'd be sweeping mud and silt and filth out of our own front doors' — as the sky cleared, the wind dropped, the storm drifted, blameless, out to sea, leaving the city battered and bemused and hanging on the phone to its insurers for hour after hour.

Images on the news showed half-submerged cars, abandoned shopping trolleys, zoo penguins basking. Café terraces retrieved their upturned chairs. Designer shops reopened, their workers chic but haggard as they mopped their marble floors.

* * *

The nuns dried off the damp lounge chairs with hairdryers and bicycled hot food up to the soup kitchen. In chapel they prayed for the world, for victims of earthquakes, of war, of famine, for flood-damaged communities in the Philippines, in China, and now here in London, who'd have thought . . . They prayed for those in temporary accommodation, for the Methodists up the road laying out camp beds and sleeping bags in their church hall. They prayed for the food bank. They prayed for Sister Imelda cycling back from Aldi with yet more tinned tomatoes. They prayed that Sister Christiane, their provincial director, wouldn't insist on going into the cellar, again, to check for flood damage — the floor was completely cracked now and no one knew if it was safe, an old building like this after a flood like that. She ought to wait for the diocese to send their building team, although the roof had completely blown off at Our Lady Help of Christians up the road, so heaven only knows when we'll see a plumber let alone a whole structural engineer . . . 'The grace of our Lord Jesus Christ . . . be with us all, ever more, Amen.'

* * *

Vespers was over.

The sisters rose quietly from the pews. Sister Josephine blew out the candles. In the doorway, Sister Christiane signalled to Agnes. The sisters watched them slip away together.

'I need you to see something in the cellar,' Sister Christiane said to Agnes. She led the way down with a torch, Agnes stumbling behind her. 'Take care on those steps — they've become even more unstable.' Agnes saw the rough brick pillars that held up the whole building. 'It was built on top of the remains of an older building, the surveyor said when we acquired it. Safe as houses, he said at the time, but then he didn't foresee God's wrath coming upon us.'

Agnes picked her way across the wreckage of the flood and wondered if she was joking. It was always difficult to tell with Sister Christiane, who ran the Hackney convent house with a mixture of maternal care and brisk authority.

But now the torchlight was strafing the cracked floor, old stone squares lifted by the water's force, erupted by the earth beneath.

'Look.' Christiane's voice seemed shaky in the gloom.

Agnes looked.

In the torch's beam, debris. A cracked china cup. Half a picture frame. A table leg, perhaps. A . . .

'Femur.' Christiane's voice was weak. 'Look. Pelvis,' she seemed to be saying now.

'Pelvis?' Agnes echoed, staring at what was, quite clearly . . .

'Skeleton. Human remains.'

Human remains. Agnes took a step closer. The bones were lying in a dusty hollow underneath the floor, now half revealed by the lifted stones.

She bent closer. There was the shape, the body, curled, on its side, the ribs, the spine, all the vertebrae linked upwards towards — 'A skull,' Christiane said. 'Just there. Still buried.'

'Oh Lord.'

Agnes crouched by the half-revealed grave. Her fingers cast tapering shadows in the torchlight beam.

'I wonder who . . .' she began.

They stood, one on each side, as if at a funeral's close.

Sister Christiane broke the silence. 'Bloody crime scene. That's all we need. Now we'll never get that roofing chap to come.'

CHAPTER ONE

It was the days before the flood. Sister Agnes sat with her friend Athena in a sunny café window, watching the Hackney traffic, the cyclists and the school-run mothers, and the teenagers swaggering and vaping at the bus stops.

They sat on curly golden chairs, eyeing trays of exquisite patisseries. Athena chatted about her life in East London, helping her boss, Simon, set up his new Hoxton outpost for his gallery. 'Weird to be in East London after Fulham . . .'

Agnes seemed tired and grey and drawn. *Older*, Athena thought, studying her. *And not in a good way. All those months in Calais, God knows I missed her, messaging isn't really the same.* But she came back, four whole weeks ago, there she was at Eurostar arrivals, a huge big hug in the middle of St. Pancras with all those couples and families and children and suitcases and someone playing one of those pianos they leave out, plonking out an Oasis number, quite unsuitable, Athena had thought, wrapping her arms around her friend, both of them smiling, hugging, laughing, linking arms, making their way out of the station and into the London air.

'Look at you, kiddo,' Athena had said, surveying her friend as they waited by the traffic lights on Euston Road.

'You survived. Well done, you. All that living in a camp with a load of old nuns.'

Agnes looked out at the people, the traffic, the every-dayness of the sunlit city. 'I wish I was still there,' she said. 'Someone has to bear witness.'

At the time, Athena had said nothing. She'd wanted to say, 'Witness to what?' but there was no doubt that Agnes had changed and it was difficult to reach her.

Over the weeks since, she'd gleaned bits here and there.

'I was useful in Calais,' Agnes would say. 'People came with nothing. We gave them food, shelter. Hope.' She would point at images on her phone. 'The boats,' she would say. 'The dinghies. People desperate to cross the Channel. And no one asks them why.'

She had come back earlier than she wanted, her tenure there cut short. A tale of rule-governed charity trustees, some interfering female executive — Agnes clearly couldn't stand her — and then suddenly she was told they needed to send Sister Benedict out there instead.

'And there's nothing for me to do in London,' she said. 'Sister Dominique is doing my old job at the hostel, so I'm stuck in the Hackney convent house. They've put me in the archives to help with the cataloguing, just to shut me up, I reckon.'

'What exactly happened back in Calais?' Athena asked, but Agnes was silent, tight-lipped with the injustice of it all.

Now, sitting in the early spring sunshine, Athena watched her friend. Athena crossed her legs in their high-heeled boots and cream, tailored trousers. She adjusted her silk scarf and waited for Agnes to comment on it like in the old days, and she could say, 'Guess what? Charity shop, darling, and it's Hermès — who'd have thought? I don't usually bother with charity shops, but some act of fate must have drawn me in and at least my twenty quid went to those darling puppies, or was it the air ambulance? There are so many of these things now, aren't there, what with the high street suffering . . .'

Agnes was gazing into space.

'Sweetie,' Athena said. Agnes turned to her. 'Kitten — what is it?'

A thin smile. 'What's what?'

'You're different. Since you came back.'

'In what way different?' Agnes smoothed her hair and Athena wondered if there was more grey amid the brown, and whether to suggest advice about hair colour and maybe a neater cut — *that short look is all very well, but it's a bit of a mess . . .*

'Unreachable,' Athena said.

'Am I?'

'Yes.' Athena felt emboldened. 'It's like you're still there, back with Sister Wilfrid or whatever she's called—'

'Winifred.'

'Your new best friend.'

'Oh, not you as well.'

'What?'

'Father Julius said yesterday that Sister Winifred seems be the repository of all my fears. Which is why I don't tell them to him.'

'Oh.' Athena glanced up as the waitress brought their coffee — smiled, thanked her. 'Julius said that, did he? Well, perhaps he speaks for us both.'

'And anyway, it isn't Winifred — she's a trooper. I was glad to be at her side.'

'So she wasn't the cause of you being sent back?'

'No. Absolutely not. But we couldn't argue with the charity trustees. Obedience. It's a bloody bind. What's so funny?'

'Oh, sweetie, I wasn't laughing at you,' Athena said, as a perfect raspberry tart arrived, with two forks. 'It's the idea that anyone could make you swear obedience. Those old nuns think they can move you all round like chess pieces. It seems to me they should play to your strengths — you're great at the hostel, and now some other old biddy is there and she's living in your flat, and you're stuck at the convent house in Hackney of all places . . . Now what's funny?'

6

'The idea of Sister Dominique being an old biddy. She's about twenty-three and fab and the kids love her, and she and our co-worker Aysha are like they were separated at birth . . .'

'Well, my point is the same. What are they getting you to do? Something in the archive? The idea of you being a librarian, as if you were a Virgo or something ridiculous.'

Agnes sighed. 'You're right, of course. There are all these old books and stuff. And paintings, that's the real problem, icons and things, no one knows how old they are. Some were already in our library, a few came from the convent house in Sussex before it closed. We've had to get this couple in, experts apparently, to do the valuation.'

'And then what? Sell them to the highest bidder, knowing your lot.'

A small smile.

'And then you can go back to the camps. Not that I want to lose you again.'

'I don't think they'll let me.'

'Why not?'

Agnes sighed. 'Two reasons. One was an incident — a drowning. A group of young men set out to cross the Channel in terrible conditions and one of them drowned.'

'One of those boats?'

'Yes. Anyway, no one knows what happened. Found further down on the coast. The others were rescued by the French coastguards and brought back.'

'Why is that your fault?'

'I knew the young man who drowned. His sister . . . she was left behind. Inconsolable.'

Again, the distant, weary look.

'But—' Athena tried. 'That's not your fault, is it?'

'No. I know that. But then—'

'It's the cow in the posh coat, isn't it?'

'The coat?'

'Pure English worsted. That's what you said. In the middle of all that mud and rain and concrete.'

'And poverty.'

7

'So what happened?'

Agnes sighed again. 'Paula. She's the other reason. She's very high up. Runs the financing of it all, here and in France. And I got on the wrong side of her. No idea what I did wrong, but suddenly I was called back here.'

'And Sister Wilfrid?'

'Winifred. She did what she could, but this woman is more powerful than we are. So I had to go.'

'And your Order?'

'They're only part of the outfit out there. They run the day centre, the kitchens. That's all. Nothing they could do.'

'So you're back with the old books.'

'Yup.'

'It won't last.' Athena flicked a cake crumb across the white tablecloth. 'You'll out-Agnes them all.'

'Thank you.' Agnes eyed the raspberry tart. 'And how are you finding East London?'

'Oh, sweetie, don't get me started. I wish I'd never agreed to help Simon with his offshoot gallery. I mean, in West London it's proper art. In Dalston, it's all weird sculptures made of old tights and filthy trawler netting hanging from the ceiling. And the place is only half built and I'm supposed to be up ladders fixing hooks into the picture rail. And I hardly get to my own flat. I'm mostly staying with Nic at his loft space in Shoreditch, which is okay, in fact.'

'Is it?' Agnes looked dubious, Athena thought.

'I know we've never really lived together, it's true, even after all these years, and I was a bit wary too. But he's put in a very nice en-suite — all that money working for that digital design company, plus a bit of my Greek inheritance, so at least it's civilised now. But, apparently, his godson Emil is coming to stay, something about doing a doctorate in particle physics . . . or was it international diplomacy?' She tucked a lock of hair behind her ear. 'Nic says I never listen, but that's because it's never anything important. Anyway, I suppose it'll be fun being around a young physicist — or diplomat — and at least if I'm here I can keep an eye on you.'

'True, that. We need our friends,' Agnes said. 'And anyway, Winifred can't possibly be my best friend. She's too . . . oh, I don't know. Teutonic. Blonde.'

'Ah. Right.' Athena flicked her long black hair with her pink-painted nails.

'And she wouldn't have just cut that cake and handed half to me without even needing to ask,' Agnes went on, taking a small forkful.

'I can see that.'

'And if she was sitting where you are now, she'd be grey and tense and weighed down with the sins of the world, bless her, whereas there you are, all cream and smart, and with that really fab shade of lipstick, and, look, it's a bright sunny day and this cake is great — shall we get another one rather than sharing this?'

Athena smiled.

'Nice scarf,' Agnes said.

* * *

'You seem better,' Father Julius said, later that afternoon. 'Athena, was it?'

Agnes tucked a small pale turquoise carrier bag behind her chair.

'How is she?' he asked.

'Fine now. I've persuaded her that Winifred isn't my new best friend.'

'Oh, what a relief. Well done, her.'

Agnes smiled.

'Gin, was it? Fizzy wine?'

'Coffee and cake,' Agnes said.

'And some more for later, I see.' Julius eyed the carrier bag. 'Even though it's Lent.'

'A millefeuille, that's all. I'm so tired of convent English puddings.'

'It's nostalgia. All your sisters did English boarding schools.'

9

'Julius, dear, I did English boarding school too, but that doesn't mean I develop Stockholm Syndrome when faced with a steamed sultana sponge.'

He laughed. 'And how is the archive research?'

'Okay if you like that kind of thing, I suppose.'

'Oh, Agnes, you are so grumpy, so you are.'

'Sister Josephine is in charge of it; she's clearly very fed up about having to explain it all to me. And there are these two archivists, a couple, Josephine was telling me. I haven't met them yet. They're art dealers, valuation people. Experts in Victorian stuff — they were recommended by the old nuns in Rouen. One of them, the wife, is originally from a local London family, according to Josephine. Anyway, their task is to catalogue everything, all the books, and there are a few actual paintings too, and some old Russian icons. It turns out all this stuff was locked away in cupboards for years, as well as the stuff from the Order's house in Sussex before it closed. Apparently this couple are appalled at our neglect. Josephine says I'll see when I meet them.'

'Icons, eh? Lucky you. They must be lovely things.'

Agnes gave a small shrug.

'Icon painting, it's a spiritual act. Not just producing art, but meditating on our Lord.' Julius turned towards the window. Sunlight filtered through the leaded arch and Agnes saw the worn red carpet of his study, the mahogany desk with its old landline phone, a neat pile of leather-bound books, his laptop, the thick oak door that led through to his church.

He had white hair, a lined face, and blue eyes which twinkled with laughter behind his gold-rimmed glasses.

'What?' he said, turning back to her. 'Having a think about how we've aged? That's what you usually do. Or at least, how I've aged.' He turned back to the window as a flurry of feathers clattered against the gutter. 'Oh, these pigeons,' he said. 'Nesting again.'

'Age,' she said. 'Both of us. We've come a long way since we met in France, all those years ago.'

'And you'll tell me I rescued you.'

'You did.'

'And here you are, a nun. Stuck with a load of old icons, a grumpy fellow sister and a couple of lordly art historians. Can't imagine you've got anything to thank me for.'

She smiled. 'No doubt, when this library task is finished, they'll find me something else to do.'

'And meanwhile, you do as we all do. Wait in quiet obedience. Though in your case, I fear, anything but quiet.'

She laughed. Julius was gazing out of the window. 'You know, sometimes I see this woman in my churchyard. You know where it's all overgrown? She arrives with a small child most days. Sometimes early morning, sometimes at dusk. I try to speak to her, but she doesn't seem to speak English. I tried Spanish, but that didn't work. That's my two languages. Unless I give Latin a go.' He smiled. 'They're gardening. Planting seeds. Her and her little girl. Determined. She seems frightened of me, so I smile and leave her alone. There's a little clearing now — you can see it. All those brambles uprooted, all the bindweed gone. A seed bed.' He sighed. 'So many of us making a home however we can, even in the dust.'

He turned back, settled at his desk. 'And talking of dust, I've got this funeral to do. Mr. Nolan. A lovely old chap from the parish, he died last week, just slipped away in his armchair. He was eighty-six. Big Irish family, they all adored him. They want me to say the eulogy as there are so many of them. There's a son, a half-sister, lots of cousins, there's even a great-granddaughter though she's only small. They reckon it's better coming from me.'

'And will you do it?'

'Och, yes, Agnes. It's an honour. You know he was a printer, originally. Came over from Ireland for work, started in the leatherworks but ended up in the big presses up the road there. Before they closed.' He smiled. 'Another way of telling stories, like your icons there. Of course, these days, we've got the internet. All that endless chatter. Not sure it'll survive in a convent archive, though.'

* * *

Later, Agnes walked back to the convent. The sun had gone, obscured by heavy clouds, and the rain was rough against her face. People scurried with umbrellas as the flood waters gathered, threatened.

From the shores of Boulogne, a dinghy set sail.

CHAPTER TWO

It was the days after the flood. The cellar was roped off with tape; half the convent was out of bounds with police officers stationed by the door. People came and went, with hazmat suits and cameras, and fragments of dust in plastic bags carried like jewels in velvet.

Sister Christiane waved her phone at Agnes. 'Look, Sister. All over the news now.'

Agnes read the headline: *Human remains found in Hackney convent.*

Sister Christiane slapped the phone onto the office desk. 'Here we go. Prepare for the paparazzi.'

* * *

'It's just a Victorian house,' Sister Imelda said to the reporter who'd knocked on the door, wanting to be shown round.

'You don't look like nuns,' he said, eyeing her skirt, her apron, her short hair. 'Don't you wear those things — habits?'

'We're Ignatian,' she said.

'Right,' he said, shifting from foot to foot on the doorstep. 'Go back centuries, do you?'

'We've only been here twenty years, we all had to move from Sussex, from the old manor house — we'd been rattling around there, rather — and anyway, we can be more useful here in the city.'

'Right. So, the dead body,' he said. 'Where was it found?'

'The Order acquired the house next door,' she said. 'We knocked through, some years ago, to make the new wing. The cellar is in the old bit.'

'Don't suppose I could come and have a look?'

Sister Imelda gave a merry laugh.

'Ah,' he said.

'With the coroner,' she added. 'Nothing to see now.'

'Right. Ancient, is it?'

'Probably from the Second World War, they think. This house barely survived the Blitz.'

'Still,' he said. 'Unexplained death?'

'You'll have to wait for the police report,' Sister Imelda said, and he found himself on the front step as the door closed firmly with him on the outside.

'I mean,' Sister Imelda said to Agnes, smoothing her apron. 'Christian hospitality is all very well, but those potatoes for lunch won't peel themselves.'

* * *

'Ooh, it's so exciting,' Athena said on the phone. 'Real bones? Like on those TV shows where they're digging up some ancient Roman place and then they find someone's wife and he thought he'd got away with it, but what with DNA and everything he's bang to rights, such fun . . . Gotta go, I'm halfway up the scaffolding and my heel is caught in a rung . . .'

* * *

In chapel, the sisters sang. '"Mightier than the sound of many waters, mightier than the breakers of the sea . . ."'

14

On the way out of chapel, Agnes checked her phone. There was a message from Winifred.

Can you ring me?

She found a quiet space in the office.

'How is it since the flood? And your dead body — I heard all about it. Reporters everywhere?'

'Yup. How is it there?'

'Wet. Biblical rain. Thing is . . . a weird thing. Paula — you know, Empress of All? She's gone to London. Suddenly.'

'Paula? Why?'

'No idea. But — she may visit you.'

'Me? Why?'

'She said, in passing, about having a coffee with you while she's there.'

'But—'

'I know. You'd think, having got you safely out of the way, she'd be happy to leave you there. But she was checking the address of the convent, typing it into her phone. "*Hackney*," she said, like it was foreign.'

'That's so weird. Paula, here? After all we've been through?'

'You're still angry,' Winifred said. A statement of fact, not a question.

'I'm working with it, trust me.'

She could almost hear the smile from Winifred.

'She doesn't even like me,' Agnes said. 'Why on earth come here?'

'Something about a trustees' meeting in London. You know what she's like.'

'I'll just make sure to be unavailable.'

There was a silence on the phone.

'Ah, I see. She's still holding the purse strings.'

'Just be polite, Agnes.'

'It will take all my resolve,' Agnes said.

Another silence.

'And how is it there?' Agnes said.

'Oh God, I miss you. So much need — all we can do is provide hot meals, space for people to be given food and hope, just for a bit. Allowing the women a space of their own in the centre. And to watch their hope dwindling. You know that young woman, the one whose brother drowned — she seems to have stolen a boat and vanished.'

'Stolen a boat?'

'A dinghy. Even in the storms we've had.'

'I remember her. Medodzi. A bundle of grief. And rage.'

'A suicide risk if ever there was,' Winifred said. There was a brief pause. 'If she was desperate enough to get into a boat on her own . . .'

A sudden crash of memory. The coastguards arriving in the yard, their trailer muddied and streaked with rain, a heap of old tarpaulin on the back. And then, the urgent French, the explanation of their find. 'One of yours,' they'd said to Agnes. 'Found him down the coast, two or three days dead, we reckon . . .'

'Are you there?' Winifred broke the silence.

'Yes.' Agnes took a breath. 'Another one for Paula Gerrard to lie about,' she said.

'What does she call it? "Reputation management." Like she's talking about share prices, not human lives.'

'And you're telling me to be nice to her?'

'Agnes, we have no choice.'

'I know we've taken vows of obedience but this is pushing it a bit, isn't it?'

'There's heavenly obedience. And then there's the world. And here we are, in the world. Heavens, this rain — it's bucketing down. I'd better go. Keep me posted.'

* * *

The library was quiet in the late afternoon and Agnes sat alone, typing handwritten lists of books into the computer. The library occupied the first floor of the extension and was spacious and light, with curtained bay windows and warm shaded lamps on the pale green walls.

She listened to the rain. She thought about a young woman setting sail, alone, in a stolen dinghy.

A suicide risk.

She stared, unseeing, at the screen.

The coastguard trailer had bumped over the gravel of the yard before coming to a halt. The tarpaulin had been roughly draped over a tangled heap, from which on one side had trailed an arm, a hand, its fingers sticky with sand.

And then a woman's voice had split the silence as Medodzi appeared, shouting and crying, flinging herself at the trailer. She'd grabbed the hand, holding it to her cheek. 'My brother,' she'd said. 'My brother, my Gedeon, my life . . . Look.' She pointed at his arm, now uncovered, at a long-healed scar along the skin. 'My only life,' she was saying, as Agnes went to her, her arm around her shoulders.

'Come,' Agnes said. 'Come away,' but the young woman was rigid, wailing, clutching the cold, stiff fingers to her face, to her lips as she shouted.

'You did this, all of you, what kind of life is this . . .' Agnes tried to lead Medodzi away, but she was pointing at the scar. 'This,' she said. 'This from a hook, long ago, when I was a child and there was fish to eat, enough for us all, sitting in the sun and eating, and even then he'd say, "Medodzi, I shall look after you always . . ." And now look — the promise he made, he never broke it, but here—' she stared wildly around her — 'here all promises are broken.'

Agnes prised Medodzi's fingers away from the clay-cold hand. She laid the hand on the man's chest. Then she wrapped her arms around Medodzi as the young woman wailed, sobbed, wept, there on the unforgiving ground as the blank-faced warehouses stood around.

The authorities eventually released the body for burial. There was a makeshift funeral. Agnes stood with Medodzi in the local churchyard, listening to the fragments of a Mass, aware that the young woman standing next to her was somewhere far away.

* * *

'Perhaps it's a saint, your bones.' Julius placed a mug of tea in front of her. Behind him the rain splashed against the dusky window panes. 'Holy relics, Agnes — your community can charge everyone to come and see.'

Agnes settled opposite him at his desk. 'It's most likely twentieth century. Maybe took shelter during the Blitz. Hardly a saint.'

'It's never stopped us before. All those relics of the true cross changing hands for folding money.'

'Julius, you're not taking this seriously.'

'Oh, but I am. And so, clearly, are you.'

'It's weighing us all down, to be honest. The bones may have gone, but they're making their presence felt. Convent life can be moody at the best of times, but there's a kind of heaviness about the place.'

'Ghosts, perhaps.'

'Now you're teasing me again.'

'Not at all. You and I know both know there's a thin membrane between this world and the next, surely.'

She smiled.

'But let's stick with the facts. How are the police doing?'

'The tape's gone, but the cellar is still declared unsafe. Now there's DNA testing, all that. They have to determine how long the body's been there. It's all anyone talks about.' She took a sip of tea. 'How's the eulogy for Mr. Nolan going?'

He fiddled with the mouse mat on his desk. 'I had a strange visit yesterday. His nephew, Seamus, nice man, helped with our website. So, I says to Seamus, "The thing with a story like this is that at least we know the ending." But he says to me, "Don't believe a word of it. What have they told you? All nonsense. Happy marriage, was it? I bet they've never mentioned the other woman. And his son?

Totally estranged. Ran away to Canada — you won't see him getting on a plane for the old man." Well, I didn't know what to say. "I've got to tell the man's story in front of the whole crowd," I said to him. "Well, you'll be telling lies," he says to me.'

Julius stirred his spoon around in his mug.

'What will you do?'

He laid the spoon down on a spare saucer. 'I'll do what you do, Agnes.'

'And what's that?'

'You know that thing you said once, about getting a shivery feeling when the truth is near?'

'Did I?'

He nodded. 'It was when something had kicked off at the hostel last time, and the police were involved, and you had a feeling that the wrong story was being told. And then someone came to see you, a woman, and started talking, and you had a shivery feeling, you said. Like this was the heart of the matter, there in front of you. Well . . .' His desk chair squeaked as he leaned back. 'I'll just have to wait for that. And then that way, when it comes to the day, in the church back there, at least I won't be telling lies.' He looked up. 'And how's the post-camp trauma?'

'Sister Winifred says one of our clients stole a dinghy from the gangs and set sail in the flood. On her own.'

Julius straightened the mouse mat.

'Medodzi,' she said. 'I knew her. It was her brother who drowned.'

The mouse mat had a bright floral design with the words *Good Vibes Only*.

'In this weather?' He looked up.

'That's our fear,' she said.

'The death of hope,' he said. 'And our stories of a loving God sit rather thin.'

She was staring at his mouse mat. 'A present?'

'My parishioners always seem to know what I need,' he said.

CHAPTER THREE

Patricia Westlake breezed into the library next morning in a bustle of know-how and spring sunshine. She seemed to sparkle in the brightness, although Agnes wasn't sure if that was her neatly pinned red hair, her loud embroidered tunic, or just her enthusiasm for the task in hand. 'So glad the Order had the sense to call us in,' she said, 'so often these muddled old collections are just stuffed away with no one to vouchsafe them, no one to oversee the necessary work . . . Donald will be here in a minute, he's just organising some decent coffee.'

The morning brightened further.

Patricia went on, 'Sister Josephine was working on this pile here, just listing the stuff, most of it rubbish, but there's the odd gem. You don't mind carrying on, do you? She's a godsend, to be honest, but you sisters are spread so thinly these days and there was something about visiting the sick, and off she went. Ah, good, here's Donald.'

The library door opened and a tray appeared, followed by a tall man with a lined face and surprisingly thick dark hair. Agnes went to help him. 'No, really, I can manage . . . Oh, I say, that's awfully kind of you — don't want the whole thing to go headlong, do we? Yes, Pat, I did indeed remember sugar, not that it's good for you — didn't the doctor say you should cut down, not that you'd ever listen to a word anyone says . . .'

Between them, they placed the tray on a side table.

'This is Agnes,' Patricia said. 'Our replacement sister.'

'Josephine out doing her good works again? Just as well someone is.' Donald smiled at Agnes and handed her a mug of coffee. 'There's milk if you want it. And poison.'

'He means sugar.' Patricia scooped two spoons of sugar into her coffee and stirred it briskly. 'Never done me any harm so far.'

'So, what's today's task?' Donald picked up a cup of black coffee and went to the heap of files. He took a spectacle case out of the pocket of his corduroy jacket.

Patricia sighed. 'Every time I think we've made progress, and then look — another crate of the stuff. What was your Order thinking of, stashing this stuff away like that?'

Agnes tried to remember Sister Christiane's briefing. *Now you're back, you can be useful in the library. We have to do a stock-take for the insurance — such a nuisance, half the stuff we've no idea what it is — and then there's the archive from the move. Do you remember — all those boxes from the Sussex house and the silly old Hawker bequest? We were just following orders, but the diocese is right, there are valuable things and we don't really know what's there . . .*

'And now with this flood,' Patricia was saying, 'you really need to get all this valued. I mean, not the rubbish, those tatty Victorian prayer books, but things like this.' She held up a large book, bound in red leather with gold lettering. 'It's about your paintings, particularly the icons, and also the books about the icons. Someone's gone to the trouble to list them all, in perfect ink. Look.'

Agnes dutifully put on a pair of white gloves. The pages were thick, with rows of neat black ink against the creamy paper.

'Donald and I have been going through the collection, trying to match them up. There are some old prints, very beautiful. And then, the actual works, those icons hoarded away in that cupboard. That's what Josephine has been working on, trying to match the painting with the entry in the book, so we get some idea of its provenance. Some of this stuff could be extremely valuable, and I have to say it's typical of this kind of outfit that no one knows.'

'Pat, darling, they have other preoccupations—'

'Oh, you can't pin it all on God, dear. Do you remember when that trust sent us off to that great big house in Derbyshire — not a single member of that family would have known God if they'd bumped into him on one of their mahogany staircases, but it was just the same kind of mess as this. We had to consult our colleagues in Berlin, do you remember? I think the BM acquired several in the end.' She tapped a pointed finger on the book's cover. 'In the past, you see, people just roamed around the world bartering for any old thing that caught their eye, that's the problem. And it's up to us to put that right.'

Donald smiled at Agnes. 'Just say yes,' he said. 'That's what I do.'

* * *

Later she would say to Julius, 'You'd have been proud of me, doing as I was told — in the end just writing lists dictated to me by Pat, as I'm supposed to call her. It's quite clear that at some point our Order housed a sister who was either a world expert on Russian-icon painting or an inveterate hoarder of poor-quality copies. Pat and Donald are trying to work out which. There are three icons listed that they say are rare and important. Pat unlocked two of them so I could have a look. One is a male saint, probably Thomas. The other is a whole scene from Revelation, loads of angels and lions and things. The third one is missing, but there's a colour photograph of it. It's the Annunciation — there's Mary and the Angel, so beautiful. The halo is barely there, it's as if the artist wanted her to be ordinary rather than saintly, Pat said, almost as if it's a portrait. But it's gone astray, Pat explained, and then she stomped about grumbling about nuns, but she does that all the time as far as I can see . . .'

* * *

After lunch, Sister Christiane found Agnes again. 'The police are here,' she said. 'At last. Some news about our bones. Could you attend to them?'

Agnes put down her tea towel. She took off her apron, aware of the glances, the unspoken question again: *Why Agnes?*

A good question, she thought, as she walked slowly from the kitchen to the office. *Why does Sister Christiane always choose me?* There was probably a long answer too, which would contain words like 'questioning', 'rational', 'evidence', 'methodical', 'difficult', 'outsider', 'never-quite-settled-to-being-part-of-our-community' . . .

Words I might reflect on, she thought. *If I had time.*

She pushed open the office door.

A woman stood there, small, in a neat navy suit and with short dark hair.

The woman put out her hand. 'DS Sandra Campbell,' she said. 'I'm the investigating officer.'

Agnes took the hand. *You're not in uniform*, she wanted to say.

'You're not in uniform,' Sandra said.

'Ignatian,' Agnes said. 'We don't wear a habit.'

'Ah.' They exchanged a smile.

Sandra sat down. 'Your mother superior said I should talk to you.'

Agnes sat down opposite her. 'Yes,' she said. 'She does tend to do that.'

'It's just an update, really, on the very strange find in your cellar after the flood. Are you ready?' Sandra smoothed her skirt on her lap. 'I mean,' she said, 'it's not just old bones anymore.'

'Go ahead.'

'So — our labs have done quite a bit of work. We're waiting for the more detailed stuff, but, so far, we know it was a woman and she died within the last fifty, sixty years or so, we think. She almost certainly didn't have children, they reckon. Also, no visible sign of injury. But the point is—' Sandra paused — 'we have to rule out unnatural death. Like, if there was a perpetrator. Depending when it happened, it makes your cellar still potentially a crime scene.' She looked at Agnes. 'You don't seem surprised.'

'No. Because the alternative is that someone who has left no trace crawled into our cellar to die of natural causes. It's very unlikely.'

'You'd make a good copper,' Sandra said.

Agnes laughed. 'Doesn't usually go with being a nun.'

Sandra smiled. 'Both in uniform. Or not.'

'Both following orders,' Agnes said.

'Or not,' Sandra said.

'And I suppose . . .' Agnes thought of the bones in the torchlight. *Both uncovering mysteries*, she was about to say.

'Except,' Sandra said, 'we police, we stick with the facts. No room for faith.'

'What about hunches?' Agnes said. 'I've seen it on the telly.'

Sandra laughed. 'You can get it very badly wrong, in my view.' She glanced around the room, at the wooden crucifix on the wall, the framed icon of the Virgin Mary placed by the old telephone. 'See, the lady in your cellar. No one can tell me she left no trace. Someone has lived, someone has died. There'll be clues. That's my job. Establishing the truth. Facts. Not faith.'

'I can see that,' Agnes said.

Sandra glanced at the crucifix again. 'It must be different for you lot. Shut away in here.'

'We're not exactly shut away,' Agnes said.

'The world still comes to you, you mean.'

'Yes. It does.'

Sandra nodded. 'True, that. And here we are — a dead body right under your floorboards.' She settled in her chair.

'So, we're doing soil analysis — that London clay might hold a few clues about when exactly she died. And carbon dating, to be more specific about her age.' She looked again at the crucifix. 'It's weird,' she said. 'We had one at home. On the wall like that. Almost exactly the same. Brings back memories.' She gave a small laugh.

'Were you religious?'

She sighed. 'Religious? My lot behaved like they'd invented it. I had no choice. Mind you, I loved it, when I was little. The stories, the singing. My nan would take us to church, me and my brothers. But after a while I began to wonder. Like — did Jesus really love me? And who was Jesus anyway?' She looked across at Agnes. 'I mean, telling you all this—'

'Go on,' Agnes said. 'These are very good questions.'

'And then . . . I was ten — not long after my birthday — and we got a kitten. Sheba. I loved that cat, and I was stroking her and I thought, no one can go telling me there's a big man in the sky doing all this. I looked at her little face and I thought, the way I feel about this little one, I don't need it to be about God, or Jesus, or anyone. And when I had that thought, I had a feeling too and I knew in my heart that it was true.'

She leaned back in her seat. 'Sister, it was a crisis. All the time in church, everyone telling me that the big man in the sky makes everything all right, and Jesus, whoever he is, knows all my thoughts — and I knew they were lying to me. I kept it secret, scared to tell my nan. And I feared my mum's rage too. But all the time, I'd be thinking. About the way I loved that cat and my brothers and my nan — and I'd think to myself, what if it's just human beings? What if that's enough? We know about love, in here . . .' She touched her breastbone, then took a long breath and smiled. 'I shouldn't be saying them things to you, Sister. It's disrespectful.'

'Not at all. It's the same here. Doubt,' Agnes said. 'We walk alongside it. If we think we know the truth, we're wrong.'

Sandra gave a brief nod. 'That sounds hard won, Sister,' she said. She gathered up her bag. 'Like I said—' she smiled again as she got to her feet — 'you'd make a good copper.'

Agnes followed her out to the hall. Those words again. 'Questioning', 'evidence', 'methodical'. She turned to Sandra. 'So the next stage is . . . ?'

Sandra smiled. 'Being a copper again? The next stage will be more from the labs, like I said. And detailed DNA stuff. And tracing missing persons. The problem is, it's quite a transient population round here, always has been. But something like this, people get to hear about it. I'm sure you've had all sorts knocking at the door. If you could keep your ears open, keep an eye out — someone might have some information.' She handed Agnes a printed card. 'That's my mobile,' she said. 'Keep in touch.'

* * *

In the late afternoon, Agnes returned to the library. Sister Josephine was there alone.

'They've gone off to find a decent cup of tea,' she said. 'Fortnum's, probably. They don't think what we have counts as tea.'

Agnes wondered if she was joking, but Josephine wasn't smiling.

Outside the sky was dark, an early twilight hastened by the returning rain. The memory of recent floods weighed heavy in the dripping trees.

Josephine was wearing a long dress in simple grey cotton. Her pale brown hair was edged with grey, and tied back in an elastic band. 'And you know,' she said, 'Patricia is born-and-bred Hackney, not that you'd tell from how she talks. They live in Wiltshire now, her and Donald. A big house. All that buying and selling.' A twitch of disapproval, a glance at the windows. 'God, this rain. What if it never stops?'

She went to the long teak desk where the crates were spread out. She pulled a pile of sales catalogues towards her and flicked through the shiny pages. The two icons, encased in glass, were laid out on the polished table, the photo lying next to them.

'She showed you, then.' Josephine's voice was thin.

'Yes.'

Josephine hovered over the works. 'And one missing. The Order has been terribly negligent.'

'Patricia hopes we can track it down.'

Josephine's lips tightened. She looked down at the two icons. 'What she doesn't understand is, they're stories. And they're prayer. The writing of them,' she said. 'Or painting. The Greek word is the same.' She touched a white-gloved finger on the glass. 'The spirit works through you. They're not art like we'd think of it.'

Agnes looked at the vision of Revelation, winged lions, golden haloes.

'That's what those two don't understand. It's not an act of self-aggrandisement,' Josephine went on. 'It's the opposite. Icon writers, or painters, saw themselves as channelling the spirit. Deliberately ego-less.' She gazed at the images. Rain dripped against the windows. She picked up the colour photograph. 'This one,' she said, pointing at the Annunciation. 'The handmaid behind Our Lady — she's spinning wool, look. She has a spindle of red wool and she's dropped it, in shock, because of what the Angel has said. It was a theme — you see it quite often in Russian ones like this.'

'Patricia said it might be a portrait,' Agnes said.

'What does she know?' Josephine twitched the photo back into the file. 'Nothing. She's an art historian. She only knows about value.' She jabbed a finger towards the icons. 'Portrait, indeed.' She picked the two glass frames up in her white-gloved fingers and placed them carefully back in the cabinet. 'She shouldn't be getting them out and showing them to anyone who passes either.' She turned the key in the lock and pocketed it. 'Here they are and here they'll stay now, if I have anything to do with it.'

Downstairs a bell tolled.

'And now it's vespers,' said Josephine. 'Not that I can concentrate. All those years we spent praying, while that poor woman was lying dead in our cellar. It just seems very wrong indeed.'

She got up to go. A fierce swish of her skirts, a slam of the door as she left the room.

* * *

'For what man can learn the counsel of God?
Or who can discern what the Lord wills?
For the reasoning of mortals is worthless,
and our designs are likely to fail . . .'

Agnes stood with the others in the chapel. The beams of the high white ceiling flickered with the candlelight.

Her mind wandered. She thought of the bones in the cellar. She thought of DS Sandra with her kitten, the child's revelation that love is enough. She thought, with a spike of rage, of her yearning to return to Calais, her sudden unexplained dismissal.

'. . . for a perishable body weighs down the soul,
and this earthly tent burdens the thoughtful mind . . .'

And now Paula wants to visit me. Paula, with her language of targets and accounts, of reputation management and business aims.

'They aren't numbers, our clients here. They're people,' Agnes had said to Paula in one of their meetings. Paula smiled with that odd, pitying look she had.

'Who has learned thy counsel, unless thou hast given wisdom
and sent thy Holy Spirit from on high?'

And then there was their last meeting: 'Oh, Sister Agnes, we're so sorry to lose you . . .' Paula had been brisk and polite. And lying.

'Why?' Agnes had asked. 'Why send me away now, when I can be so useful here?'

'If it was up to me,' Paula had said, 'of course I'd love to keep you. But you must understand, we're all part of a team here and I have to do as I'm told.'

Another lie. The idea of Paula doing as she was told.
Now, Agnes intoned the verses, her voice tight with rage.

*'Glory be to the Father, and to the Son, and to the Holy
Spirit . . .'*

In her mind, a young woman, alone in a storm.
A hand trailing in the mud.
A woman's bones in the ground beneath her feet.

*'As it was in the beginning, is now, and ever shall be, world
without end . . .'*

'Amen.' The women's voices echoed in the quiet, still
space.

* * *

The nuns left the chapel in silence, in darkness, as the candles
were extinguished and rain still rattled the windows. They
departed to their rooms, their private places.

Agnes found herself alone.

She moved quietly along the darkened corridor,
unlocked the door to the cellar, placed her feet silently, one
step at a time, on the rough wood stairs.

The torch's beam cut across the lifted flagstones, the
grave-like empty space. She smelled the sour, dank smell.
She saw the black stains against the walls where the flood
had left its mark. She saw traces of the tidying, the brushing,
the forensic gathering of earth into plastic bags, as if the dust
itself might have a tale to tell.

'Who were you?' Her voice was flat against the cold
stone walls. 'And why? Why was this your last resting place?'

There was silence. Only the trickling of distant gutters.
She wondered what she'd hoped to find.

On the floor, debris — a broken china cup in blue and
white, an ornate vase, chipped and chunky green. A brass
photo frame, empty and bent out of shape. Half a chair leg.

'Someone has lived. Someone has died,' Sandra had said. 'No one can tell me she left no trace.'

Until we wash up on a beach with only a scar to tell of who we were.

Agnes climbed back up the steps, headed for her room along the shadowed corridors.

CHAPTER FOUR

The blustery early April gave way to a warm, settled week of spring, the city air pricked here and there with fleeting floral scents. The community settled into Lent with psalms of sinfulness and grief, and meatless meals.

The diocesan surveyor arrived, at last, stepping briskly through the house and tapping on a laptop as he went. 'It'll all dry out in due course. Might want to take the opportunity to fix the damp in your laundry room. Good structure, these terraces, not like the older stuff. That posh house on the corner — you know, the one that sold for a small fortune — the water came halfway up the walls. A chap I know in the trade got called in for the insurance claim, they've got a fight on their hands, I can tell you . . .'

* * *

The news spread of the convent bones. Local people had theories. There were callers — a man certain it was the holy relics of a recent saint. 'Perpetua, not that old one, the other one, Hackney girl . . .'

A woman, one rainy morning: 'I can tell you who she is. My friend does seances and she had a message, from a lady who has not gone beyond. She told me the spirit was saying, "Held against my will, but now the truth is out . . ." I promised Deirdre I'd knock on your door and tell you how it is . . .'

'Thank you so much,' Agnes had said, ushering her towards the door, wondering about her shabby raincoat and her muddy wellington boots. 'Thank you so much . . .'

'Another one?' Sister Imelda looked out of the front window, watching the woman in the raincoat struggling to light a cigarette. 'I had a man claiming he'd been swapped at birth and our woman in the cellar was definitely his mother.'

* * *

In the library that afternoon, Patricia was scathing. 'People will make things up, won't they? I blame all this crime stuff on the television these days. I bet she wasn't killed. Silly mare just went down there to die, and now everyone's turned detective. Oh, and there's a man downstairs asking to see a nun and once again you're the only one around. Where on earth has Josephine got to? They really ought to have a recruitment drive, these nuns of yours . . .'

* * *

'A sister, are you?' The man was standing in the hallway. 'I need to talk about the bones.'

He looked frail, tapping on the floor with a long, polished cane as he followed her into the office, carrying a leather briefcase. But, Agnes realised as he sat down, he wasn't old — his hair still thick and brown, his hazel eyes bright. His breathing was shallow and he waited for it to settle. 'I'm sorry,' he said, as if he always started a sentence that way. 'Interrupting your day.'

'Don't be sorry,' she said. 'It's fine, really.'

'I wasn't sure whether to come, grasping at straws really. It all seems rather insubstantial . . .' He bent to the case as he spoke. It was worn and brown like his tweed jacket, exuding quality and age. He fiddled with the catch, then produced a faded cardboard box.

'This,' he said. 'Probably useless, but I heard about your lady in the cellar and I felt I had to speak. Audio tape,' he went on. 'Probably no use, no way of listening to it now . . .'

He lifted the lid from the shallow box. Agnes saw a round plastic reel.

'Quarter-inch tape. It was how we used to record things,' he said. 'Now you just point a phone at someone, and the quality's much better too.' He managed a thin smile and his eyes brightened.

'My father,' he said. 'Colin Tillman. He was a man of letters. A writer, and a translator of Russian. Quite well known in his day. He made these recordings for his memoirs, unpublished in the end, a long and sad story, but anyway . . .' He straightened his shoulders. He seemed younger now, a blush of colour on his cheeks. 'The name on this box, I remembered it. And I remembered what he said about her, and this house before it was a convent — and I thought, what if this is her?' His voice was raised. 'And I thought, I can't leave these things unsaid, his voice unheard, if she's lying there, under those stones.' His gaze shadowed as he looked up. 'Celia,' he said. 'That was her name. If, indeed, it is her.'

There was a silence. Somewhere a clock chimed the half-hour. Agnes heard someone approach, a soft tap of footsteps fading away again along the corridor.

'We know very little about her,' she said.

He nodded. 'I read about it. A woman, probably in her forties, died sometime in the middle of last century.'

'Yes,' she said. 'You've been following the case.'

'I had to,' he said. 'If it is her — there is no one else who knows.' He looked up. 'My father was a Communist. Long after everyone had given up on it, he still believed. But more than that . . . there was a scandal . . . he might have been a spy. People turned away from him. The memoirs remained unpublished. My mother . . .' He stared down at the floor.

'My mother was disappointed in him. Actually—' he looked up — 'not just in him. In most things.' Again, the almost smile. 'And he had a lover.' He pushed the box towards her, and Agnes saw, on the plastic reel, a dusty label, on which was written, *Celia*. 'Celia Danziger,' he said. 'His *grand amour*, I'd say.'

'Was it . . . secret?' Agnes asked.

He shifted on his chair. His thin legs uncrossed then crossed again. 'In the end, he wanted someone to know about it. That's what I think. Else, why keep all this?' He waved towards the tape. His fingers were long and delicate, with one silver ring on the middle finger of his left hand. 'He could have destroyed it all, with all the letters.'

'There were letters?'

'When the scandal broke, when people began to cold-shoulder him, he was very angry. He said the accusations weren't true, he was a linguist. "I studied Russian to understand Dostoevsky, not to bring down the West," he'd say loudly. He began to clear things out, boxes of stuff thrown away.'

'To hide evidence?'

'I thought that once. But in the end, I think it was just pure rage. The bits and pieces that were left, none of that incriminates him. But, you know, a Russian speaker during the Cold War — he loved Russia, its culture, its literature . . . and then, to fall in love with Celia, who claimed to be descended from Russian aristocracy . . .' His breathing was faster now and Agnes saw the effort of his unaccustomed speech. 'And in those days, he had friends in the establishment, he moved in literary circles; someone might have asked him the odd favour — talk to someone, note down what they say, *you speak the lingo, dear boy* . . . he might not have realised what he was doing and he was sympathetic to Moscow — it might have looked like he was trading secrets.'

'And Celia . . . ?'

He shrugged. 'An unknown quantity where all that is concerned. I met her once. Twice if you count an unexpected encounter. She wasn't chic, or beautiful, or anything like that. She had a sort of vulnerability about her. She was quite shy — maternal to me, kind. I liked her.'

'And . . .' Agnes gathered her words. 'And what makes you think she was buried in our cellar?'

* * *

'Maybe Russian,' she said later on the phone to DS Sandra Campbell. 'Would have died in the seventies if this Frank is to be believed. Yes, Frank Tillman. His father Colin used to visit a house in this road and Mr. Tillman thinks this Celia woman would have been there too.'

'The seventies,' Sandra said. 'The carbon-dating results would agree with that. Go on.'

'Frank said this Celia disappeared. His father thought she'd left him, but then after a while became convinced she was dead. His letters were returned, unopened. He was heart-broken, Frank said. He tried to start afresh, he was planning to go and live in France, but he never got there. Lung cancer, diagnosed much too late. Frank's mother, Janet, she went to live with her sister in Bournemouth, stayed there some years before she died too . . . Sorry, what? Oh, yes, Celia Danziger. Possible Russian descent. That's all I know,' Agnes said. 'And the tape's here if you want it.'

There was a silence, then Sandra said, 'Fifty years. In which case, it's still a crime scene. I mean, if there was a perpetrator, they might still be on this planet. On the other hand, there are no signs of violence.' Another pause. 'It's a question of whether your lady becomes archaeology or criminology.'

'Ah. Okay.'

'History examines the clues to find out who she was. Us coppers, we're asking the clues to tell us who intended her to die.'

'But still a mystery,' Agnes said.

'A different sort of revelation,' Sandra said. 'I'm glad that man came to see you. We'll have a chat with him. And in the meantime, keep me posted.'

Agnes rang off, stared at her phone. The image of Frank, snapping shut his case, taking her hand and placing the box containing the tape in her palm with that reluctant smile, getting slowly to his feet, leaning on his stick as she opened the front door for him. On the steps he had turned to her. 'I've done my bit,' he'd said. 'I'll talk to the police as you suggest. I just didn't want to leave her there, unknown. Unmourned.'

Behind him, the trees swayed in the gusty wind.

'If it is her,' he said.

'Well,' Agnes said, 'we've had all sorts of people claiming it's a ghost, or a holy relic of a saint. At least a Russian spy is believable.'

He laughed then.

'And,' she said. 'How do I listen to the tape?'

'That's up to you. I heard it once, when my father was dictating it. I don't want to hear it again.'

'And — how do I contact you?'

'My card is in the box,' he said. 'With the tape.'

He descended in slow, careful steps. She watched him walk away, hesitant on the wet pavement.

* * *

'A Ferrograph,' Julius said, later that afternoon. 'That's what you need.'

'A what?'

'A reel-to-reel tape recorder. To play this thing.' He touched the tape box with a fingertip. 'Can't wait to hear the whole story,' he said. 'Russian spies. A great love affair. A disappointed wife in Bournemouth. And Dostoevsky — it's got it all.' He smiled at her. 'Do you think this chap was making it all up?'

'At the moment, nothing would surprise me.'

'I suppose it's no more unlikely than the holy relics of St. Perpetua of Hackney.'

Agnes took a sip of her coffee. 'And where do I get this Ferro thing?'

'Ah.' Julius frowned into his mug. 'Good question. We had one once, when I shared the vicarage with that deacon from Norwich. He must have taken it with him when he went back. Typical Anglican.'

'Anywhere nearer than Norwich?'

He smiled. 'Leave it with me. You've got the whole of *Dr. Zhivago* on that tape, I can't wait to hear it. It'll take my mind off dear old Gerry Nolan. I've now got another version of his life, did I tell you? His half-sister came to see me. He was almost convicted for fraud, it turns out, a property scheme in Galway, but she rescued him with a small inheritance of her own. I mean, how is that going to fit? I mentioned her to Seamus, the nephew, who just said, "Don't believe a word that woman tells you."'

'You're enjoying it, Julius,' she said.

He shook his head, looked up at her. 'Your shivery feeling is more difficult than I thought.'

* * *

'When this house wasn't a convent,' she said to Patricia at the end of the day, 'what was it?'

'Well, next door, the corner house, was derelict, before your people acquired it. But this bit . . . what was it Donald? Some kind of meeting place.'

'Did you know any of them?' Agnes asked.

'Oh heavens, no,' she said. 'Not our kind of people at all. Bolshies, you know. With their scruffy little newspapers.'

'Are you sure, dear?' Donald said. 'I thought it was a vegetarian café in those days. Full of architects and people.'

'My point exactly,' Patricia said. 'Now, where have we got to? Donald, dear, pass me 1964, will you?'

CHAPTER FIVE

'I'd be careful, kitten.' Athena spread butter on a piece of toast. 'She might be radioactive if she was killed by the Russians — you know what they're like.'

Agnes laughed. 'It was a long time ago.'

'Yes, but that stuff they use — it lasts for centuries, they say. So, what do you think of Nic's loft?' Athena gestured to the sturdy beams, the wide, bright, sunlit skylights.

Outside, a weekday morning, the buzz of traffic, the cooing of pigeons. *A sense that all is well*, Agnes thought.

Even though it isn't.

'He's transformed the place,' Athena was saying. 'Done it all himself. This kitchen is fab — who'd have thought he'd have understood where the dishwasher should go? And there's enough space for us not to annoy each other. Well, almost.'

'And the godson?'

'Emil, he arrived yesterday. I was right, it's microbiology. But he has a sideline in magic.'

'Magic?'

'Tricks, you know. "Pick a card." That stuff. Making pennies appear from people's ears. He says it's a good earner, people hire him for parties and things.' She stirred her latte in its long glass. 'He's sweet. Claims to be twenty-five but he looks about seventeen. Thick blond hair like Nic — well, like Nic before he lost half of it, but don't tell him I said so. They're not related, though. Emil's dad was at school with Nic.' She took a sip of coffee. 'So this bird was the lost love of a funny old spy? I can see Julius would get all twinkly about it, I can just imagine.'

A chirrup of a text interrupted them.

Agnes picked up her phone, read it, put it down again.

'More nuns?' Athena licked her spoon.

'Winifred. Paula's definitely in London. Some high-level meeting with finance people. And for some reason she wants to see me.'

'The witch from the camp?'

Agnes nodded.

'Ah, I wondered what was wrong. I thought, either you're worried it's going to pour with rain again, like we all are round here, every time it drizzles — have you noticed, people stop and stare up at the sky as if waiting for a sign? — or,' she went on, 'it's the fact you're all still living in a crime scene. I'm not surprised it's weighing you down. And then I was thinking, why you?'

Agnes blinked at the question.

'I mean, why do all those nuns think you're the one who's going to sort it out? Your mother superior always bustles in your direction whenever there's a problem.'

Agnes smiled at the thought of Sister Christiane bustling. 'Provincial director,' she said. 'We don't have mothers.'

'Well, that's something, I suppose. But you can't be the only nun there who's able to string two sentences together when faced with the outside world?'

Agnes reflected on this. Sister Madeleine, a stalwart ally, currently working at the school in Yorkshire. Dear Dominique at the hostel, with her haute cuisine and Little Simz blasting from her earphones. Old Sister Phyllida, now in sheltered accommodation, although it was the rest of us who needed sheltering from her lectures on Old Testament theology . . .

'It's not that,' she began. 'There's Sister Imelda, but she tends to be busy with the kitchen, and there's Michaela, but she's sorting out the music we need for Easter, and there's Birgitta from Denmark, but she's still a novice . . .'

'Backbone,' Athena said, rather surprisingly. 'That must be it. This bustling non-mother of yours knows that whatever life throws at you, you'll answer back. And in times of floods and buried skeletons, I guess that's what's required. And now this mare from the camp is coming over and I bet that's part of it. You must have challenged her in some way.'

Agnes sighed. 'You're right, of course. I just wish I knew what I'd done.'

'She's met her match in you. That's the problem. She won't let it lie.'

'She's like a robot,' Agnes said. 'When she talks, it sounds like a script. As if all her language comes out of some kind of management training in damage limitation.'

'And all those posh coats.'

'Perfect make-up too. In all that mud.'

'Weird. Though you can tell a lot about a woman from her lipstick.'

'She goes on about brand management.'

'Oh God, I know these people. All so entitled.'

Agnes looked at her.

'They're always coming into the other gallery, asking Simon about values and futures and auction prices, but when he asks them about artists and what they like, they've no idea. Though Simon's so good with them. "The customer is always right," he says.'

'Well, if it means he can open a second gallery in Hackney . . .'

'Oh, kitten, those types aren't going to come all the way to Hoxton. They all drive those cars you're always stalking online — Mercs or Audis or whatever you're secretly coveting at the moment, I know what you're like — and their satnav wouldn't even recognise the postcode. Unless they really think there's a future value in draping their brand-new

40

conservatory with used underwear.' Athena stood up and gathered her coat. 'I need to go to work. Let's meet for lunch tomorrow, sweetie. I want to hear all about your radioactive spy.'

* * *

Agnes headed back to the convent for kitchen duty.

She was aware of shouting — two men, on the corner. One was sandy-haired, wearing a suit. He was standing by a large car, gesturing towards a house — the posh house, she realised, the one the surveyor had mentioned.

'. . . completely ruined,' the man in the suit was saying. 'You've got one bloody job, you can bloody well do it.'

The other man was wary, his hands in the pockets of his smart raincoat as he took a step back. 'I can see you're upset.'

'Upset? I'm bloody furious. We put our life's savings into that house; my wife had her heart set on living there and now just because it rains—'

'Not just rain—'

'Don't you dare say act of God. Don't even start.' The man by the car was shouting. His hands were now in fists at his side as he took a step forwards.

'I'm not prepared to be threatened by you,' the other man said. 'I shall make my report as described.'

'Extortion, that's what it is. Call yourselves insurers?'

At this point, the car door opened and a woman stepped out of it. 'Adam, you're upsetting the baby,' she said. She was wearing a loose trouser suit and a silk scarf floated at her collar.

He ignored her. 'History, that house has got. That's why we love it. It was here long before all this new rubbish—' he gestured around him — 'and it'll be here long after. Those wool traders knew a thing or two about building to last and I won't be told otherwise.'

The woman seemed on the point of tears. 'Adam, please . . .'

A baby's cry came from the car. He glanced towards it.

'Mr. Crosland,' the man in the raincoat said, 'I will do what I can.'

'You'd better do.'

'I'll be in touch.' The raincoat man acknowledged the woman with a nod, then turned and walked sharply away along the street.

The man held the car door open for the woman, and then they both got in and drove away.

* * *

'Wool traders?' Agnes thought, mounting the convent steps. She thought about the icon handmaid with her spindle of red wool. She wondered when Hackney was ever known for wool trading. Probably never, she thought.

* * *

Later, her phone rang, loud in the convent kitchen. Julius.

'I've got it,' he said.

'Got what?'

'A tape player, of course. I asked that parishioner, you know that museum curator, the tall one with wispy hair, always sings the hymns louder than everyone else — sure enough, he appeared this morning with a huge machine. It's sitting here. He showed me how to work it. Come over whenever those nuns can spare you.'

'Lunch,' Agnes said. 'I'm on duty.'

'Well, after that. If you can survive the sultana pudding.'

CHAPTER SIX

Agnes sat in Julius's office. The low afternoon sun filtered through the dusty windows. They both stared at a large, grey, metal machine. Its cord was plugged into the wall. A chunky light said *power*.

'Well?'

Agnes handed him the box. He lifted out the tape and threaded it through the heads, then connected it to the other reel. 'What's funny?' He looked up.

'You are so keen on this.'

'God's work, Sister. Isn't it?'

She laughed. 'Or just avoiding your eulogy family.'

'Oh . . .' He shook his head and sighed. He put his hand to the switch. 'Okay? Here goes.'

A turn of the switch and the two reels began to move.

Noises. A clunk of a microphone. A male voice.

'Um . . . this is . . . hang on, can't tell if the blasted thing is on. Right. Well, er . . . where was I? Ah, yes. I was saying, if they're going to write me out of the story, if I'm forgotten . . . a crime, it would be. They're wrong, you see. And they know it too. But no one has the guts to admit it.'

The voice was reedy and clipped, its old-fashioned tone roughened by the hiss of tape.

'I have nothing to atone for. Nothing at all. My fear is that I will be remembered for something I am not. Or, worse, that I will be forgotten altogether. My work by definition would never be of global renown . . .'

At this point there was a crackle, as if the tape was damaged. Agnes and Julius heard fragments.

'. . . prize for translation . . . my love of the Russian language . . . eminent in my time, reviewed in the important journals . . . "Tillman brings to the discipline a new and youthful voice . . ."'

The words degenerated into an inaudible, muffled litany.

Julius switched it off. 'I don't want to damage it.'

'Do you think it's the machine?'

He peered at the tape head. 'No idea.'

'Shall we ask that museum curator?'

He shook his head. 'Absolutely not.'

'Perhaps wind on a bit?'

He wound the tape on and pressed play again.

The reedy voice continued, restored.

'. . . atonement. Not for my work, for my friends, not even for my son. But for her. I will never understand why she left. Not a day goes by when I don't ache with longing for her. There. I can say it out loud, alone here, with just you, my whirring witness, at my side. I miss her. And as the weeks go by, as they lengthen into months, I fear the worst. For some time I imagined her happy and carefree, living a new life elsewhere, a sunny shore, a cocktail in her hand . . . but now, as the silence thickens with no word from her at all, I fear that she lies dead and cold, and that I will never see her again . . .'

The tape rolled on, but there were no words. A clunk, perhaps a sob, another crackle. Julius pressed stop, wound forward, pressed play.

There was music. A faded piano sound, a female voice as if from a recording. '*God shall wipe away all tears*,' the voice sang, '*. . . all tears from their eyes . . .*' There was more, the words inaudible, the piano out of tune. Then it stopped. The tape wound on, but there was only silence.

Agnes and Julius watched it turn. The tape ran out and flapped round and round, unleashed.

He switched it off.

He leaned back in his chair. 'Well.'

She looked at him.

'You do bring all sorts of people into your life,' he said. 'Hmm.'

'Gospel singing,' he said. 'That song. God wiping tears away . . .'

She picked up her tea mug, stared into it. 'If only He did.'

* * *

'No, no, no.' The voice on her phone that evening was emphatic.

'Frank,' she said.

'I don't care. I've done what I came to do. The police know her name. And you have the tape. Clearly, from what you say, he's talking about Celia. And all that stuff you say, about him being misunderstood. Typical of him. He made such enemies and they were always the ones to blame. I came to you because I feared that I was the only person in the world who knew about that poor woman in your cellar and I felt I should do the right thing. I have no other tapes, nothing. There is nothing else I can do to help.'

'It's in terrible condition,' she said. 'There's bits of music.'

'And how can I help with that? The last thing I want to do is hear that man's voice again.'

She looked out of the window of her convent room at the black branches of the trees, the small, square shimmerings of distant windows.

'What you need to know . . .' His tone softened. 'I never really knew my father. None of us did. Except perhaps Celia. He was a private, hidden person. I've had to do a lot of work on myself . . .' He stopped, then went on. 'Work out who I am, separate from what he wanted me to be. I don't wish to be drawn back in. Do you understand?'

'I understand better than you know,' she heard herself say.

'Ah.' There was a smile in his voice. 'Nuns. Yes, of course.'

'Well,' she said after a moment. 'Thanks for the tape.'

'Thanks for understanding.'

Another pause and then a click.

She looked at her phone screen. She put it down.

I am no further on, she thought.

A dead woman, now in a fridge in a coroner's mortuary. And the world wants answers.

But who the hell was Celia Danziger?

* * *

'Perhaps he killed her,' Athena said the next day, as they sat in the café on the corner. 'Not the Russians at all.' She prodded a focaccia sandwich. 'Oh God, all this rocket. Can't stand the stuff.'

'Perhaps who killed her?'

'The father of the mysterious thin man. Perhaps this whole tape business is a cover.'

Agnes watched Athena pick rocket leaves out of her sandwich. The café was busy, its striped awning sheltering the outside tables from the angry wind. 'You can have some quiche; I won't eat all this,' Agnes said.

'Okay.'

'If he'd killed her, this Tillman Senior—' Agnes divided her quiche into quarters — 'why sound so upset on the tape? I mean, really upset. It didn't sound fake.'

'Hmm. Dunno. But weird it's all in fragments, like, not really giving anything away.'

'Julius is going to ask Josh, his nice young tech man, about it.'

Athena laughed. 'You've given him an interest at last. Well done, you. I've always thought Julius could do with something, poor man, having to sit there on his own with only God for company, or Jesus, maybe, and all those needy parishioners. He's so sweet with them all, but really he needs to get out. I thought, it's not as if he'll do yoga or marathons or join a choir or a quilting group — but this is ideal.' She reached across and speared a quarter of quiche. 'And you say the son didn't want to know?'

Agnes took a sip of coffee. 'You know what it's like. He's in the second half of his life, and he's managed to make something of himself, and I reckon he's had therapy, and the spectres of his highly strung father and disappointed mother have faded into the distance — he doesn't want to bring all that back.'

'Oh God, kitten, don't we just know that feeling?'

'I just wish he could dig out more tapes before he goes back to his life.'

Athena stirred her cappuccino. 'Perhaps he killed your woman in the cellar? The son.'

'Then why get involved?'

'But that's what they do, double agents. Pretend one thing in order to cover up what they really are. In the stories, anyway.'

'But this isn't a story. This is real life. Just some poor woman who died alone and before her time, and was only brought to light by the flood.'

'Then it's her story, isn't it? That's what you need to tell.' Athena eyed the rest of Agnes's quiche.

'Go on,' Agnes said. 'I had breakfast.'

CHAPTER SEVEN

The afternoon had settled into a bright spring sunlight. The library was light, with its pale green walls and teak wooden panels, after the dark of the convent corridors.

Agnes found Patricia in a theatrical mood.

'Now, this one.' Patricia was waving a large hardbacked book, pointing at a colour plate. Her hair was swept up in an orange turban, and she was wearing turquoise dungarees and white ankle boots.

Behind her, Donald winked at Agnes.

'. . . the seven seals,' Patricia was saying. 'Look. Very like the one you have here. Sophia, goddess of wisdom, obviously an ancient figure co-opted by the early church. And she has seven pillars of wisdom and each pillar has seven seals. All very numerological.'

'The Book of Revelation,' Agnes said. 'That's where it comes from.'

'Oh, I know that.' Patricia tucked a lock of hair into her turban. 'Your people cobbled together all kinds of things and called it Christianity.'

Donald smiled. 'My wife believes the sixth century was only a few years ago. You have to get used to it.'

Agnes took the book from Patricia and laid it on the desk.

'One of many things about my wife that take some getting used to.' He pushed his glasses further up his nose, turned the pages of a book.

'Take no notice,' Patricia said. 'He adores me really.'

'Nearly as much as she adores me,' he said.

Patricia tutted and went back to the shelves. 'Oh, and by the way,' she went on, 'this Communist cell you mentioned . . .' She held up a book, squinted at the cover, blew some dust from the pages and placed it on the table. 'Of course they weren't really Communists by then, were they, Donald? No one with any sense would have been by then, but I suppose that kind of person still likes to play at things. But anyway, Donald was looking through the old crates in the corner there and he found these. Some ghastly old copies of the *Morning Star*, a few Bolshevik pamphlets, aren't they, Donald, dear? Of course, all in a terrible muddle like the rest of this stuff.'

Donald handed Agnes a small pile of papers. 'Actually,' he said, 'a very interesting little book about social housing, *Machines for Living In*. Lovely little designs, look. Nothing about planning a revolution that I could see.'

'Oh, Donald, you're betraying your sympathies again.'

He smiled. 'It's not my fault you can't tell the difference between Bauhaus and Bolsheviks.'

'Both as bad as each other.' Patricia inspected another book.

Donald was leafing through the papers. 'Anyway, the point is, there were these. Photographs. Look.'

Patricia handed Agnes a pair of white gloves. 'Can't imagine they're anything to do with your poor woman in the cellar, but, just in case, you might like a quick browse through them.'

Agnes put on the gloves. There was a photo album, faded leather and worn pages, most of them empty. Tucked away loose in the front were a few black-and-white photos. Five, in total, as Agnes spread them out on the table. Two people standing somewhere rural, both with bicycles, both smiling. A view of a mountain. A postcard of a Swiss village, blank on the back. A very young man, apparently surprised by the camera, turning his head towards it, waving it away. And a photo of an icon, an Annunciation — the Angel, Our Lady, her lady-in-waiting dropping her spindle of wool . . .

'Patricia,' Agnes said. 'Have you seen this?'

Patricia held the photo by its edges. 'Hmm,' she said. 'So difficult to see in black and white, but — it does look like our missing one, doesn't it Donald?'

Donald peered at the photo. 'I say, old love. Looks just the thing.'

Patricia sat down with a heavy sigh. 'It's all such a muddle. We were told we were cataloguing your Sussex collection. But it seems that half this stuff was already here, completely uncurated, no accession numbers, nothing. I know you nuns all have other concerns, but I do think someone could have made the effort, frankly. And now there's this woman in the cellar and everyone's distracted.'

'It's not at all surprising, dear—'

'I had someone at my pottery class asking me about it at the weekend, as if it was some kind of murder mystery.' She placed the photos back in the leather album. 'And it's clearly upset Josephine, we've hardly seen her. Which is a shame, because actually she's fearfully good at all this. A great asset. Her cataloguing is expert and her knowledge really quite extraordinary. I said to Donald, anyone would think she'd studied it in a previous life, rather than being shut away in a nunnery all these years.'

'Patricia, dear, they're not shut away. I mean, Agnes here has only just come back from a refugee centre in France.'

Patricia's bright gaze alighted on her. 'Really?'

'I did tell you,' Donald said.

'Refugees? You mean, like in Calais? Those poor people crowding onto those awful boats? What were you doing?'

'We ran a kitchen,' Agnes said. 'Providing hot food. Also a centre for the women and children.'

'Ah, the children. It breaks one's heart, it really does.' Patricia paused and flicked at a book with her yellow duster. 'What is it that lovely poem says, you see it quoted these days, about how no one will put their children in a boat unless the sea is safer than the land. Something like that.' She placed the book in a crate, drew out another, puffed the dust from the spine. 'Well,' she said. 'Jolly good you were doing something useful at least.'

Agnes and Donald exchanged a glance.

Patricia folded her duster into four. 'And when you see Josephine, do tell her we could really do with her here, won't you?'

* * *

Back in the office, Agnes looked at the three photos she'd taken away. The two people with bicycles, the man surprised by the camera. The icon, its original gold and scarlet flattened into black and white.

Fragments, she thought. None of it adding up to a whole story. Just broken bits.

Perhaps that's how all lives end. The living breathe a shape into their lives. But then it's over.

Like Julius's attempt at a eulogy for the many lives of Mr. Nolan.

She wondered about phoning Frank again, suggesting — what? That he look at the photos? If these are his family, he won't want to know. And for all I know, they're nothing to do with him.

She thought of the voice on the tape, the ache of longing for the missing woman. She wondered what it would be like, to feel that kind of yearning.

God shall wipe away all tears, she thought.

She placed the photographs in an envelope and stuffed them to the back of a drawer in the desk.

* * *

At dusk she was sent to the post box for Sister Christiane. She walked through the warmth of the spring evening wondering what Winifred was doing, how the food supplies were going, whether the rain had ceased there as well as here.

She passed the corner of the old wool house. She thought about the floodwater coming halfway up its walls, that angry man shouting at the insurance investigator.

The angry man was there again. He was sitting on the front steps, smoking a cigarette. He briefly looked up as she passed, then bent to his phone again.

* * *

The next morning was sodden with rain. Agnes sat in the office with a to-do list. She checked some emails, placed an order for more candles, sorted out the foodbank rota.

The day wore on. The police appeared outside, taking away the last of the blue-and-white tape.

'That's better.' Sister Imelda watched from the office window. 'It was getting rather unsightly.'

'Unsightly?' Agnes was counting petty cash into the housekeeping box.

'Flapping in the wind like that. At least now we can pray for the soul of that poor lady in peace. Whoever she was.'

The mood in the convent lifted. At vespers, the dripping of the gutters — so recently a portent of disaster — became instead a quiet accompaniment to the chanting of the psalms.

And so it was the following morning when Agnes, back in the office, was interrupted by a persistent ring of the doorbell.

Frank stood on the steps, his stick in one hand, two large, ancient plastic carrier bags at his feet. He looked up.

'Ah, good,' he said.

She picked up the two bags.

In the hallway he stopped, his breath coming in short bursts. He brushed rainwater from his shoulders. Then he said, 'I was lying.' He gestured to the two bags at his feet. She could see a box of thin cardboard, spines of books.

'More stuff,' he said. 'Writings. Another tape. He was obsessed with being unforgotten. These are they. I want nothing more to do with it. You can have them. I never want to see them again.'

He seemed more thin, more weary. 'I didn't sleep last night,' he said.

She looked at him. 'Come and sit down,' she said.

He shook his head. 'This is all I know of this sorry business.' He waved a fist at the boxes in the bag. 'I've no idea what's on them but you can have them. Back at the house there's film, too, Super 8, it says on the boxes. There's probably a projector somewhere, but Sister, I'm done with it.' He leaned hard on his stick. 'The police contacted me, as I knew they would.'

'I'm sorry—'

'No, no need for sorry. You and I, we're good citizens. The story must be told. They took a statement, said they'd try not to bother me again.' He raised his head. 'I had a father. He wasn't perfect but he was the only father I had. He had a story, which I was part of. I was his son. It was good enough for me. There was my mother, and there was Celia. I knew all that.' He stopped, caught his breath, went on. 'I am grateful that there is someone to hear the story. But as far as I'm concerned, it's over. He was a scholar. An intelligent, private man. He had his work. He had his wife, he had his great love, and he had me. You must understand, Sister . . .' He was leaning against the wall, stooped, dishevelled. 'I am not prepared to hear another story. Those days are past.' Again he pointed at the bags. 'Celia has come to light. It might have been better if she'd rested in the darkness for ever.'

He straightened himself, reached out his hand.

'I want nothing more to do with it,' he said again. 'But — thank you. I am grateful.'

'Frank — there are photos.'

'Photos?' He looked pale.

'Please wait.' She ran to the office, snatched up the envelope from the drawer.

He was standing exactly as she'd left him. She passed him the photos. He looked at the bicycle one, shook his head. Then he looked at the young man turning away. 'This is me,' he said. 'Can't you tell?'

She took the photo. She looked at his unguarded expression, the thick wavy hair, the intense, bright eyes.

'Celia must have taken it,' he said.

'It's in our archive,' Agnes said. 'Or at least, it found its way into our library.'

He leaned against the hall wall and the blinking of his eyelashes was against tears, not rain.

'Do you want it?' she said.

He shook his head. 'As I said, Sister — I'm done with it all. She was . . . I hardly knew her, but she was an old soul. That's what I'd say. An old soul. You keep it — I expect PC Plod will want to have a look. But as far as I'm concerned, it's over.'

He shook her hand, went to the door. As she opened it for him, Sister Josephine came along the corridor and he looked up. He raised his hat to her, an old-fashioned politeness from another age.

Agnes watched as he descended the stairs, tapping his stick onto the rain-soaked pavement.

Sister Josephine hadn't moved. She stared after him as he went to the end of the street, turned the corner and disappeared.

'Well,' she said, pulling her sleeves down over her hands. 'The people who come and go. Anyway, lunch to sort out.' With a nod to Sister Agnes, she turned and went into the house.

Agnes reached for the plastic carrier bags. They were wet, but the box inside was dry. She lifted them into the hall, prepared to carry them up to her room, wondering, as she struggled to take the two very heavy bags upstairs, whether Frank might not be as frail as he looked.

* * *

At lunch, Sister Josephine said, 'Who was that man?'

Agnes wondered what to say. 'He knows Julius,' she said, not entirely truthfully. 'Family history stuff. That's what the tapes were for.'

'Ah.' Sister Josephine appeared distracted by the apple crumble that appeared on their table. 'He just . . . ah, well, never mind. Can you pass the custard?'

CHAPTER EIGHT

In the afternoon she walked to the bus stop to catch the bus to Julius's church. She had borrowed a bag on wheels from the convent kitchen and packed it with Frank's two bags.

As she passed the wool house, a woman came out, pushing a buggy along the drive. Agnes recognised her from the argument with the insurance man or surveyor, or whoever he was. She had shoulder-length blonde hair and was wearing a navy belted raincoat, and Agnes felt old and shabby in her hooded anorak that flapped against the rain.

The baby in the buggy dropped a toy and squawked loudly. The mother picked up the toy, muttered something impatient and went on her way.

The number 242 bus came almost immediately and Agnes was glad as it had come on to rain again.

* * *

Julius stared at the bag on wheels as she dragged it into his office.

'All tapes? We'll be here for weeks.'

'One tape. Lots of papers and stuff. I hope that Ferro thing is still working,' she said. She took off her damp coat, brushed raindrops from her hair.

'And now Frank's saying there's amateur film at the house, though heaven knows how we get to watch that.' She began to unpack the bags onto his desk.

'Files. Papers. Oh — look. There's a book, a rather lovely one.'

Julius picked it up. It was bound in thick cream paper, printed with a broad-brush sketch in black ink on the front and the words *Krotkaya and Other Stories*.

'Dostoevsky,' he said.

'This one's in Russian,' she said, handing him a thin paperback. 'And here's the tape.'

He put the books on his desk next to a small globe, a snowstorm with a London scene. He watched Agnes thread the first of the tapes through the machine. 'Are we really going to—'

The clunk of the play button. The reedy voice. Agnes settled in her chair.

> '. . . the birth of my son was a fresh start for us. My wife, Janet, was in poor health, but she seemed to brighten in those early weeks of motherhood. I engaged a nanny, a recommendation from my sister. Frank was a sunny child and as he grew, our marriage also flourished. I began to have hope. My work also grew and expanded. An invitation from the Institute necessitated a new area of research and I began to explore further the Russian mathematician I mentioned before, helped by the interest of an English publisher in translations of his work. However, it was not to be. This period of relative happiness was set to founder against the rocks of my wife's fragile mental health and I was once again seeking out psychiatric help, while finding myself increasingly alone in caring for our son. As his needs changed from that of a toddler to that of a schoolboy, it became clear that I would be insufficient and so with my sister's help we looked for a school where he could board . . .'

Agnes switched off the machine.
'Ah.' Julius nodded.

'There goes the sunny-natured child,' Agnes said.

'I wonder when he meets Celia,' Julius said.

Agnes forwarded a bit, then pressed play.

'My wife's insistence on listening to her priest only added to her belief in her own sinfulness, and each day I watched her shrink further from the world and from me. Had I ever had any kind of religious belief, I would have lost it over those years . . .'

The voice crackled, broke into fragments, and once again another voice broke through, a deep male singing voice. *'Who's that writin'? John the Revelator. Who's that writin'? John the Revelator. Wrote the book of the seven seals.'*

The singing stopped; the tape rolled on in silence.

Julius switched off the machine. He looked across at Agnes. The windows were grey with rain, the room weighed down with the chill of it. He reached across for his desk lamp, looked up at her in the glow of its light. 'Are you all right?'

'The Book of Revelation,' Agnes said. 'The seven seals. Patricia was showing me one of the icons — Sophia, the goddess of wisdom, and her seven pillars, and one of them has seven seals . . .'

Julius rewound the tape and they listened to the singing again, the gentle gospel beat, the deep warmth of the singing voice. Again, it came to an end and Julius switched it off. He said, 'Josh talked about tape breakthrough. But maybe — maybe this isn't breakthrough. Maybe it's intentional.'

'The religious wife? Recording gospel music on her husband's tape?'

'Or he's deliberately recording over it?'

Agnes leaned back in her chair. 'There are photos with our icons, and one of them is of Frank as a young man that he said was taken by Celia.'

'So, your icons . . .' Julius said.

58

'It must be the case that some of the Russian stuff that ended up in our building is connected to Celia.'

Julius brushed dust from the edge of the Ferrograph with a fingertip.

He fiddled with his mouse mat, his tin of pens. 'You've told the police, then?'

'I spoke to Sandra. She said it's a question of whether Celia's death counts as history, not crime.'

'From my reading of the Bible, I fear they're often the same thing.'

Agnes picked up the snow globe, shook it. 'Tower Bridge,' she said. 'And the river. Your parishioners?'

He nodded. 'They look after me.'

Agnes smiled, replaced the globe. 'I'll be late for vespers,' she said, gathering her bag. 'Fragments. It's all clues to a life. And it only resolves when we die.'

'And not even then.'

'Ah,' she said. 'Your eulogy.'

He stood up to show her out. 'I've got a new mourner,' he said. 'His grief-stricken landlady. Rosetta. Originally Italian. She told me people think there were goings-on between them — that's how she put it — but she says it was never like that and he was always respectful, but then she started crying, saying he always set the boiler thermostat and now she's bloody freezing here in this English weather, how's she going to manage, and as for the fuse box . . .' He peered out into the London evening.

Agnes laughed. 'It's going to be a long eulogy.'

'I might just play our friend singing on the tape there instead.'

* * *

Agnes walked back to the bus stop. The rain had cleared, at last, and there was a scent of spring as the last of the sunset faded to dusk.

Her phone pinged with a text.

Paula. *Looking forward to seeing you tomorrow. I'll come to your convent at ten unless I hear otherwise.*

Agnes held out her arm as the bus drew up.

Paula.

She was aware of a tight clenching of her breath at the name.

What on earth does she want?

CHAPTER NINE

At ten the next morning, Agnes was in the office. The blinds twitched in the breeze from the open window; the fledglings twittered loudly in the hedge beyond the railings. Agnes closed the window, smoothed her white shirt, checked the top button again, wondered why Paula had this effect on her.

There was an authoritative ring on the doorbell. She heard the murmur of a nun — Sister Birgitta, quiet, welcoming — and then the door opened.

Agnes stood up. Paula seemed to stoop under the doorframe, swathed in a large purple coat in tailored wool, a soft grey scarf at her neck, an arm outstretched.

'Agnes.' She smiled.

Agnes shook her hand, gestured to the chair opposite her own. She took in the expertly cut hair, the chic blonde-grey, the subtle pink lipstick. *Athena will want to know*, she thought. *You can tell a lot about a woman from her lipstick* . . .

'It's so very kind of you to see me,' Paula said. Agnes remembered the deliberate warm tones of her voice, as if learned — wherever she also learned her listening skills, her management-interface skills, her brand-outreach skills . . . 'You must be so busy, here, back at your HQ.' It sounded like a sneer, but the voice was steady, the smile carefully authentic.

'Would you like a cup of something?' Agnes settled opposite her. 'I'm sure one of the sisters—'

'Oh, no, no, thanks.' A wave of a hand. 'I wouldn't dream of interrupting their important work.' She reached into a large designer bag of soft black leather and drew out a laptop. She balanced it on her knees, fired it up.

Agnes watched. 'Would you like a desk, a table?'

'No, no, really. I'm fine here.'

'So,' Agnes said. 'How can I help?'

Paula sat straight-backed, still smiling. Agnes looked at her neat hair, her effortless make-up, and remembered this was how she'd looked at Calais, surrounded by chaos and mud and poverty. 'Oh, didn't Winifred say? It's just a small thing,' Paula said. 'You need to sign this non-disclosure agreement.'

'What?'

'It's just a formality, everyone who's been through our charity in France has to do it and as you've left now . . .' She typed into her laptop, passed it across to Agnes. 'You can do a signature here.' The smooth smile was unwavering.

Agnes pushed the laptop back to her. 'I don't see why I should.'

The smile faded. There was a glint of rage behind the perfect mascaraed lashes. 'But you have to.'

Agnes took a breath. 'You arranged my return to London,' she said. 'You knew I wanted to stay.'

'That's not true.' Her voice was sharp. 'Your Order wanted you back. We make sure to work very closely with our partner organisations.' She bent to her screen. 'Look,' she said, tapping at the keyboard, 'I'll print the NDA papers out for you and you can think about it — how would that work? Then I can pop back in a day or so and pick them up.'

'Non-disclosure?' Agnes tried to settle her voice. 'What on earth would I disclose?'

'You must understand, Agnes, the buck stops with me. I am the CEO. Anything to do with charity financing, I have to account to the trustees.'

'We're religious,' Agnes said. 'If anyone tells us anything, we assume it's in confidence unless they're actually breaking a law.'

'You were running the day-centre food orders. You had access to the accounts. To HR data.'

'Why should any of that be anything I'd want to disclose?'

'It's a formality, Agnes.'

'And if I don't sign?'

'Oh, Agnes, don't make it difficult again. Poor Winifred is trying to carry on the good work out there on her own. She won't thank you for being obstructive.' Paula tapped her laptop. 'There,' she said. 'All done. The trustees will be glad we've had this conversation. Life can go on.' She clicked to print.

The printer whirred into life and began to spit out pages.

Agnes took a breath. 'I heard that one of our clients got into a boat on her own. Medodzi.'

A twitch, a blink. 'Who?'

You knew her, Agnes thought. 'Medodzi,' she said again. 'Winifred said she stole a dinghy and set sail.'

'When?' Agnes heard the tremor in her voice.

'During the storm.'

The printer whirred rhythmically.

Paula smoothed her smile back on. 'It sounds like a death wish,' she said. 'I mean,' she added, 'if she didn't drown, she'd be brought back by the gangmasters. They're not ones to let a dinghy out of their sight.'

She spoke warmly as if she was talking about mutual friends, not the distant, faceless, muscular groups of men that Agnes would glimpse here and there, lounging, smoking, laughing, waiting. And she remembered that Paula was once or twice seen among them, lounging, laughing too.

It seemed odd now.

Paula leaned back in her seat. 'How I envy you all this. The peace and quiet.'

No, you don't, Agnes thought.

'I went to a convent school, you know.'

'Really?'

'Yes. Scholarship, luckily. We wouldn't have been able to afford it otherwise.' She smiled. 'Everyone around us was chapel, but my father wanted me to succeed.'

'Ah.'

Paula fiddled with a sleeve of her coat. 'Self-made, you see. A businessman, in Lancashire. Engineering work for the mills. All gone now, of course.'

'And your mother?' Agnes realised, after all this time working alongside her in Calais, how little she knew about Paula.

'Oh, she was just a housewife.'

The printer stopped.

'My sister,' Paula said. 'She's more like my mother. Still there. Suburban, you know. House, garden, family. Dogs.' She smiled.

'Whereas you?'

'Me?' She bent to the printer, began to gather up the pages. 'I think success is important. I was like my father in that way. Ambitious. I don't have any qualms about admitting that.' She reached across and handed the document to Agnes. 'I'll leave this with you. As I said, it's a formality.'

She delved in her bag, produced a small mirror, checked her appearance, a purse of her lips, a tweak of a lock of hair.

'But,' Agnes said, 'what would I possibly disclose?'

Paula snapped the mirror shut. 'Our clients have to trust that their personal information stays with the project and doesn't go beyond its information systems.' She packed her things away, got to her feet. 'All charities do it when people leave — I'm surprised your Order doesn't.' She tied the belt of her coat.

Agnes stood up to open the door for her. 'We don't leave — that's the difference.'

'You don't leave,' Paula echoed, with her odd, pitying smile.

Agnes opened the front door for her. Paula offered her hand again and Agnes felt the dry, cold fingers.

'Thanks so much for your time. I'm due back in France next week, but I'll pop back in a couple of days for that form. Good luck with all this—' she tilted her head towards the door, the house, the nuns, the work, the faith in God, the rest of Agnes's life.

And then she'd gone.

* * *

The office felt tense and scratchy. Agnes opened the window again, breathed fresh air, listened to the fledglings' chatter. She sat at the desk, feeling the space around her soften once more. She called Winifred and almost cried with relief when she picked up.

'She's been, then,' Winifred said.

Agnes could hear distant chatter, laughter, the beat of music. 'Yes,' she said. 'She's been. "Poor Winifred," she called you.'

'What did she want? She usually wants something.'

'I have to sign an NDA.'

'An NDA? That is so strange. Why?'

'No idea, she said it was a formality. Something about appeasing the trustees.'

'She's always cared more about pleasing them than anything else.'

'It was as if it was about something completely different. And then I mentioned Medodzi and she went really weird. For a micro-second, before she put her Madame Tussauds face back on.'

'Strange.'

'I mean, what on earth does she think I might disclose?'

'She's trying to bully you, still,' Winifred said. 'It's the only explanation.'

'But for what? I'm out of her way now.'

'Was she wearing that coat? The purple one?'

'Yes.'

'And those boots — they never get a fleck of mud on them and the rest of us in wellies. Can't stand the woman.'

'When I mentioned Medodzi — it's like we were talking different languages.'

'Medodzi. I fear for her, Agnes.'

'Is there any news?'

'None. I am holding her in my prayers.'

'Not something that Paula would understand.'

'She's never straightforward. She's up to something. There's an old house near you, detached, seems to be across the road from HQ. She was doing a search on it, just before she left. I checked her history. And then she put in our convent address.'

'Why would she do that?'

'Maybe she needed you as an alibi,' Winifred said.

'So,' Agnes said, 'whatever she came here for, it's about something other than this so-called NDA?'

'Always going on about working hard on behalf of our clients. Working hard on behalf of Paula Gerrard, is what she means.'

'I'd better go. I'll keep in touch.'

* * *

Agnes looked out of the window. She sipped her mug of cold teabag tea and wondered whether she could steal the Westlakes' Fortnum's supply from the library.

She heard the doorbell go and for a brief, clenched moment thought that Paula had returned. Then she heard DS Sandra Campbell's voice, heard her being shown towards the office, 'I'm sure Sister Agnes is in there . . .'

'Ah.' Sandra was warm and crisp and smart, and Agnes breathed again.

'Lots of news,' Sandra said. 'Big news. About your lady in the cellar. Your phone call was really helpful.'

'Coffee?' Agnes said.

'Your kind sister is fetching some.' Sandra settled in a chair. 'I spoke to the coroner after we talked. The labs have been hard at work. So, firstly, as we thought, we're dealing with old news. Seventies, as you said. We're standing down the murder squad. If they could ever stand up in the first place.' She laughed. 'But, you'll want to know more about her.'

Sister Birgitta appeared. She was one of the younger sisters, and she had pale red hair and freckles, and wore a Fair Isle jumper. She carried a tray containing two mugs of coffee, a small jug of milk, a bowl of sugar and two spoons. She gave a small bow, smiled at Agnes and backed sweetly out of the door.

Sandra watched her go. 'You nuns.' She shook her head. 'Like a whole damn tea ceremony.'

She picked up a mug, refused milk and sugar, took a sip. 'Go on,' Agnes said.

Sandra peered at the mug, placed it on the desk. 'Your lady there. She was white, partly Jewish, something like Ukrainian — I mean originally. Obviously, none of that might mean anything at all. By the time of her death, she was a Londoner like the rest of us.'

Agnes smiled.

'They've confirmed the details. As we initially thought, she died fifty-odd years ago. She was in her forties.'

'You know lots.'

'Our guys are good. Also, no sign of injury.'

'Right. So . . .'

Sandra leaned back in her seat. 'As I say. All inconclusive so far, but we're still working on it. We spoke to your man, and he was as helpful as could be, but we'll have to talk to him again. Then, after that, trawling through people reported missing at the time — but the weird thing, the name he gave us, no mention of it anywhere. Like, was she living under the radar? A false name? Or maybe it wasn't her. So, we're keeping on with it, but anything else that comes to light, you tell me, right?'

'Well, we've had people who say she's been visiting them as an unquiet spirit.'

'That would be great. We can give up with the guesswork.'

'But,' Agnes said, 'it must be Celia.'

'Celia.' Sandra gave a brief nod. 'That's the name he gave us too.'

'And,' Agnes went on, 'I mean, all these years, she was lying there. Buried. I just think, someone must have meant her harm.'

'You don't know our geology team. Thing is, those stones wouldn't have covered her, but your cellar has flooded before and over the years, all that silt — them foundations built on London clay, that's what shifted in the flood, according to our guys with their microscopes.' She tidied her jacket collar one side, then the other.

'Are you saying . . .' Agnes began. 'I mean, all of us here, all the sisters, we've been thinking of her as a victim.' *Even if we've not said it out loud*, she thought.

'London clay,' Sandra said. 'Keeps its secrets. I saw them Roman things at the museum. There was a ring. Gold. Emerald. The loveliest thing, like it was made yesterday.' She looked at her fingers, then looked up. 'Layers, you see. History. One century, then another, all laid down in that silt. This city keeps its stories close.'

'But someone must have buried her—'

'Sister, what our team has shown so far is that them bones had been untouched since whoever that woman was crawled into the cellar to die.'

'But — but — no one would do that? It was 1970. Why would anyone crawl into a cellar to die?'

'If I could answer that, Sister, we'd be talking the sum of human misery. And we'd be here a long, long time.'

'There are photos,' Agnes said, opening the desk drawer, drawing out the envelope. She laid out the images on the desk.

Sandra stared at them. 'Did Mr. Tillman give you these?'

'No,' Agnes said. 'They appeared. In our archive. With the icons.'

'Weird.' Sandra picked one up by the edges. 'What a nice man he is,' she said. She tapped the photo. 'This is him, isn't it? Much, much younger.'

'It connects Celia with this house. With our archive. And it connects Frank's father with all of it.'

Sandra glanced at her untouched coffee. She looked back at Agnes. 'I'll tell the team.' She took out her phone, took pictures of the photos, put them back in the envelope. 'Keep these safe,' she said. She got to her feet. She glanced back at the envelope on the desk. 'Thing is, Sister, clues can take all kinds of shapes. Oftentimes, we don't know what we're seeing. We don't see the meaning in the thing. Those photos, for example.'

'I should have told you earlier, you mean.'

'You people here, with your faith, you may be quite content to spend your life waiting for a sign that never comes. But in my job, we have to go out looking for it.'

'Another difference between us,' Agnes said.

'But a small one.' Sandra smiled. 'If anything else occurs to you, give me a call.'

The hall was in shadow, pierced by sudden sunlight as Agnes opened the front door.

'This weather.' Sandra looked out. 'You wouldn't believe all that flood we had, would you?'

* * *

Agnes went to her room, sat at her desk, the photos in front of her. Showing them to Sandra had felt like a betrayal. *Of whom?* she wondered. Of the strangely frail-looking man on the convent doorstep who carried bundles of tapes around London? Or of the woman in the cellar, a story long since buried, upended by the flood?

Agnes picked up the black-and-white image of the icon, the angel and the spindle of wool. She thought about the seven seals and 'John the Revelator'. She thought about Celia's life, its tightly woven threads unweaving.

Another chiming of her ringtone. Athena.

'Kitten, I was just thinking about you. Are you all right?'

'No,' Agnes said. 'Not really.'

'I knew it. I mean, this full moon, it's doing us all in. Frankly, it's like we're all stuck under a cloud waiting for the next storm. And did that silly mare from the camps come to see you? I bet you're completely traumatised. How are you fixed for tea tomorrow? I know what you're like, but I've found a lovely place with real teapots and a choice of about a hundred different teas, and don't go on about missing vespers or whatever it is — God may be worried about people like me, but He knows He can rely on you.'

Agnes laughed, noted the address of the new tea place, agreed three o'clock tomorrow.

On the desk lay Paula's printout. *That silly mare from the camps.' What was Paula not saying? It was as if she was waiting for some kind of reveal from me. And I've no idea what it was. And then, that tiny glimpse of worry when I mentioned Medodzi.*

Stuck under a cloud, waiting for the storm.

She tucked the photos away in her desk, pulled on her anorak against the spring chill and left the building. *A walk,* she thought. *Across the park. Breathing London air.*

It was as she was heading back for vespers that she passed the wool house. The front door was open. Someone was leaving. A woman in a purple coat with blonde-grey hair. The woman gave a brief wave to whoever was inside, then hurried down the drive and got into a sleek black taxi.

Agnes leaned against the wall.

Winifred had been right. About Paula checking the convent's address. And theirs.

Perhaps she really does need an alibi.

Perhaps she didn't need to see me at all.

The sky had clouded over. A light drizzle threatened heavier rain and there was a rumble of thunder. Agnes pulled her hood tighter around her chin and headed for vespers.

* * *

That night Agnes slept fitfully, aware of noise outside, occasional shouts, distant sirens, the revving of fast cars, a single, loud, explosive crack. *A gunshot?* she wondered, then turned over and went back to sleep.

CHAPTER TEN

The rainy night gave way to a cold dawn. The nuns filed out of the chapel in silence, the words of the Psalms still suspended in the air, the soft echoes of timeless voices praising an eternal God.

They parted into silent groups: some to the kitchen, kettle on, milk from the fridge, muesli out in bowls; some back to their rooms; Sister Christiane, grumbling, to answer the knocking at the front door, 'So early, don't they know we have prayers to say . . . ?'

Five minutes later she found Agnes in the kitchen. 'Police,' she said. 'Again. A shooting. In the house across the road, the old posh one. There's an ambulance, all those officers in their spacesuit things, look.'

They stood on the front steps, peering out into the street. Sister Christiane turned away to where Agnes stood behind her. 'I'm getting slightly tired of this,' she said. 'If they'd left us in Sussex, we could all just be sweeping leaves and weeding the garden and praising the Lord.' She looked at Agnes. 'And how dull that would have been. The Lord is indeed merciful.'

* * *

Agnes washed up the breakfast and then went out. The wool house was taped off, busy with white suits and patrol cars blocking the drive. The morning had brightened and sunlight broke through the clouds.

The door was open, with signs of movement inside.

She walked up to the front gate. Beyond, she could see the driveway, the front steps, sturdy, old and proud. Like the flagstones in our cellar, she thought. Weighed down with the past, until they'd been lifted by the rains.

The woman she'd seen before was standing by the gate, with a baby in a pushchair. The woman turned to Agnes. She was fretful, twitchy. 'I need to get stuff,' she said. 'They won't let me. I need things for this one.' She pointed to the child in the buggy. The baby was gurgling happily under the hood, waving a blue bunny. The woman was wearing a large winter coat in spite of the sun and she seemed to have pyjamas on underneath, pink-and-white striped. Her feet were in bright orange sliders. She was brittle and tearful, and now she grabbed Agnes's sleeve. 'I never thought he'd do it,' she said, and burst into tears.

Agnes held her as she sobbed. The baby was studying the bunny, passing it solemnly from hand to hand with an intense, brown gaze.

'I'm sorry,' the woman said.

'No need—'

'I don't know what I'm going to do.'

Agnes pulled a packet of tissues from her pocket, handed them to her. 'I'm Sister Agnes,' she said. 'From the convent on the corner.'

'Ah.' The woman surveyed her, dabbing at her face. 'They said there were nuns there. You had a flood too — there was a body, they said?'

Agnes nodded.

'Ours was a catastrophe, our flood. Adam never got over it . . .' She gave an odd, choking sob. 'I can't believe . . . he said he'd do it, but I can't believe he'd . . .' She turned away, her hands over her face. The baby chewed the bunny's ear.

The woman spoke again. 'I'm Stephanie,' she said. 'Stephanie Crosland. My husband . . .' She looked at Agnes. 'I found him. I'll never get over it.'

'What will you do?' Agnes said.

'I'm supposed to go to my sister's. When they let me. I've got to go with the police for questioning, can you believe it? As if I'm a suspect. All these questions, like I'm the accused, then they get all apologetic — "It's routine, Madam, in cases like these . . ."' Her eyes welled with tears. 'My sister's insisting I go to her when they let me out. I don't want to leave . . . I don't want to leave him. I need to get things and they won't let me, nappies for this one. And what about a funeral, I said, I need him back . . .' She began to cry again.

Agnes scanned the police activity, then turned back to Stephanie. She hesitated, then said, 'Paula Gerrard. Do you know her?'

Stephanie blew her nose. She blinked up at her. 'Yes,' she said. 'Do you? She's an old friend of my husband's. They go back years. She was here yesterday from France, they were catching up—'

A police officer appeared, a young man in uniform. 'Madam, we need you to come with us. If you talk to my officer there, she can fetch the articles you need.'

Stephanie touched Agnes on the arm. 'Thank you,' she said. 'Gotta go.' She pushed the buggy up to the front steps. Agnes watched a police officer wait by the baby as Stephanie rushed inside.

* * *

Agnes went to the library. There seemed to be nothing else to do.

'A death,' Patricia said.

'Maybe suicide,' Agnes said.

'Sister Josephine says that place is cursed.'

'She does?'

'Not like one of yours to be superstitious.' Patricia gave a brief bark of laughter.

'Take no notice.' Donald looked up from a heap of ancient hardbacked books. 'You may have noticed my wife has a keen sense of irony.'

'Nonsense, Donald. Not ironic at all. Curses are real enough. A collective belief system, like magic. Or religion. Perfectly respectable. That's how beliefs work. My lot knew of that house too, when we lived round here. My father was a headteacher over in Shoreditch. He used to call that house Sailcloth Towers.'

'I thought it was wool,' Agnes said.

'Wool?' Patricia cast her a crisp glance. 'Nonsense. No wool trading in Hackney. I mean, silk, yes, those Huguenots down the road. But not wool. That house, he was a cloth trader made good. Nineteenth century. Sailcloth. Stuff for the docks, sent by the canal from Lancashire. And then he goes and builds himself that ghastly mansion with silly pretend Tudor turrets. Don't know what they were thinking of. My father used to say, "I suppose if they're living in it, they won't have to look at it."'

Donald exchanged a smile with Agnes.

'But that young couple,' Patricia was saying. 'Can't think what made them buy it. And the poor man had a row with a surveyor, I gather. Enough to drive anyone over the edge.'

'It was insurance,' Agnes said.

'Even worse.' An airy wave of her ringed fingers. 'Now, Sister, would you mind continuing your listing of the old catalogue, thank you so much.'

Agnes turned the carefully inked pages. A gunshot in the middle of the night. And now that woman in her pyjamas, with the buggy and the baby. And Paula.

* * *

At lunchtime she went to her room and called Winifred.

'Why would Paula know the people across the road from me?'

'What?'

'All that stuff you said, about her looking up the address on search engines, before she came here. You were right. An alibi. It's like it was an excuse to visit the couple across the road. And now the husband seems to have shot himself, last night, and heaven only knows where a man like that finds a gun . . .'

'Agnes — you're not making sense.'

'It's all so strange. Paula asking me to sign meaningless forms, and then visiting the house across the road. And now this man is dead. Wherever that woman goes, somebody dies. Violently. Patricia says Josephine said the old sailcloth house was cursed, but I don't think that's it. I think it's that woman, like she walks in a kind of toxic cloud. I'm amazed I survived this far.'

'Agnes — who has died?'

'A man. Across the road. I heard the gunshot, in the night. At least, I think I did. It seems to be suicide. Just after Paula Gerrard calls on them. I mean, what is it with that woman?'

'Agnes, slow down a minute. This man, this neighbour. The police are on the case, presumably?'

'Yes, but — Paula was there. She visited the house. And then he died.'

'That is very strange,' Winifred agreed.

'So,' Agnes said, 'what am I going to do?'

'Do about what?'

'About everything. About Paula stalking around causing death. I'll have to tell the police what I know about her.'

'Agnes — the police will have asked the family, won't they? It's a weird connection, but it doesn't mean you have to do anything at all.'

'But she came here. Tried to make me sign stuff. I mean, I can't help but be involved. It's like Medodzi,' she said, aware she was shouting. 'Clearly, the poor girl decided she couldn't stand it anymore, and who can blame her? And Paula doesn't give a damn.'

There was a careful, listening silence.

76

'I know you didn't want to leave,' Winifred said. 'But you'd had a hard time here after the police raid. After Gedeon drowned. So, maybe, at least being back in London—'

'With shootings in the middle of the night, and Paula at the heart of it?' Agnes tried not to raise her voice.

'You can't carry it with you,' Winifred said.

'It won't leave me behind.'

Another silence, then Winifred said, 'Like I said, it's up to the police.' A small, audible sigh. 'If you really want to, just tell them about Paula.'

Agnes settled her breathing. 'Now there's a thought.' She smoothed her hair. 'You're right, of course. The poor wife is going to stay with her sister. The police have taken the body away. So, I go to the coppers and say he had an old friend who I really don't like and who weirdly appeared in London the night of his death.' She took another, deeper breath. 'It's all so strange. And meanwhile, the bones in our cellar seem to be coming back to life, all sorts of tapes and photographs about this woman who died decades ago. It's all fragments, Winifred, as if I've got lots of bits of different jigsaws and none of them join up.'

She heard Winifred's smile on the phone. 'Promise me,' Winifred said. 'Promise me you'll step back, leave Paula and her weird coincidences alone, and sit in the library making calming lists of all the heaps of junk that came from Sussex.'

'I'll try.'

'You may have left Calais behind, but we know how hard it is to shake off. We had another full-on battle last night, the CRS boys with their shields rounding up the men, the women all cowering in the day centre. Remember what I said when you left. Don't carry it with you. Leave it on these godforsaken beaches and set sail.'

In her mind, Agnes saw a blue bunny being passed from tiny hand to tiny hand. She wanted to cry.

'Okay?' Winifred said. 'It's a deal?'

'It's a deal,' Agnes said.

'What are you doing this afternoon?'

'I'm about to go to a posh tea place in Fulham and eat cake.'

'Thank God Athena's looking after you. Speak soon.'

* * *

Athena poured tea from a floral teapot into two floral cups. 'And proper tablecloths, sweetie. I knew you'd like it. You look dreadful, by the way.'

Agnes told her about the gunshot and Stephanie and Paula and the curse of the cloth house and her promise to Winifred. 'And she said, thank God you're looking after me.'

'She said that?' Athena gave a bright, surprised smile. 'Those nuns know a thing or two after all.' She pushed a plate of tiny cakes towards Agnes. 'And as for the house being cursed, I wouldn't be at all surprised.'

'Patricia the archivist said it was a collective belief system.'

'Clearly a very clever woman. And what with the moon in Saturn now.' Athena picked up a cake fork. 'Nic told me yesterday I was gullible, but I'm not, am I? I stick with the facts, me. It's like Emil yesterday, magicked my phone charger out of the microwave. I mean, how was it in there? He's amazing.'

'He did?'

'Oh, he's so cute and clever. In the lab they're working on antibiotic resistance, at cell level — he explained it all to me. And then, this morning, he told me to pick a card, any card. It was breakfast and we were making toast, and he offered me the pack. I got the two of diamonds — he didn't see it, promise — and then when the toast popped up, there was the two of diamonds, toasted into it. "Is this your card?" he said. I mean, either he's done something weird to the toaster. Or, it's magic. And I said to Nic, it must be magic — dear Emil isn't going to be tampering with our kitchen appliances, is he? And then Nic said I was gullible and Emil said that people who have a sense of wonder are special people.

78

Isn't that sweet? Now, talking of rationality, what's Paula's star sign? We need something sensible to work on.'

'I've no idea.'

'Really?' You must know, you worked with her for months. Mind you, everyone's got the wrong star sign at the moment. There's this carpenter helping at the gallery at the moment, Steve, he's an actor really but between jobs, obviously a Leo but when I asked him, he said second of March. Pisces. Can't be. Nothing watery about that man at all. I blame the pandemic — it interfered with our DNA or something.'

'Perhaps Emil's lab can research it,' Agnes said.

'Ooh, good idea, he's so clever.' Athena put down her cup. 'She's right, your wise nun. Leave it on the beaches. Don't carry it with you. That woman in your cellar had a life and now she's dead. Leave it to the experts. Look, it's spring, the sun's shining, we've eaten all those cakes and now I'm going to investigate those interesting little designer shops we passed along the road there, did you see those orange sandals in the window?'

* * *

Agnes got off the bus at Victoria Park. She walked towards the convent. Outside the sailcloth house, one patrol car stood guard.

'Promise me,' Winifred had said.

That baby, gurgling under her pram hood. And now fatherless.

Paula's allowed to have old friends in London.

Leave it on the beaches, Winifred said.

She turned the corner, and found herself face to face with a young woman. The woman was tiny, scrawny, her black hair in tangles, her dress torn, her rainbow-coloured trainers muddy and unlaced. Agnes reached towards her, cried out her name, but the woman flinched, whirled, and then ran, fast, disappearing into the park and the sunlit trees.

CHAPTER ELEVEN

Agnes sat in her room, looking at her phone. She heard the distant city bells chime midnight.

She punched up Winifred's number on her phone. It went to voicemail. 'She's here. Medodzi. I've seen her. She ran. I chased her. She got away. Winifred, don't ask me to leave it on the beaches. Because the beaches have washed up right here. In London. In my street.'

She put her phone on her desk. She looked out at the urban night, the streetlight pixellated in the sheeted rain.

Why didn't I grab hold of her, seize her, give her somewhere to stay, a place of safety?

A memory from the camp.

'A place of safety, Sister? And where would that be, then?' The words had been mocking, a tight smile on Medodzi's young face as she'd waited for Agnes to speak. There was wood smoke and diesel fumes, the smell of cooking, the beat of music, a mosaic of lights from phones. Beyond the warehouse concrete, the darkness, the containers, the shingle. The sea.

Safety.

And what would I have answered?

Earlier that day there had been a police raid, massed flanks of riot shields amid the smoke and the mud and the

80

rain. Shouting, running and the crunch of fists, jeering and shoving, and the cries of pain, the slam of van doors as the men were rounded up, the women hiding, shivering, hugging their children close.

Later, the men released. Bruised, limping, returning from the fight.

'Soldiers into battle,' Medodzi had said. 'My brother, that's what he thinks. That's what scares me. He'll fight back. That's why we need to leave. We need to go.'

A place of safety, Agnes tried to say. Medodzi looked at her. 'You call this a place of safety?' She shook her head. 'No way. Me and my brother, we know what safety is. And we will keep running until we find it.'

And then, days later, the grey-cold hand trailing broken fingers through the sand. And in the still silence, a woman's voice. 'My brother . . .' The body lifted onto a stretcher, one arm stiff at his side.

In the aftermath, Medodzi ceased to speak. Agnes found her, one afternoon, tried to offer her a plate of food, rice and chickpeas. 'You must eat,' she said.

A shake of her head.

'Medodzi . . .'

'What is there to live for?' The girl had turned to her, her eyes large in her hollowed face. 'My brother's gone. Together, we travelled all this way. For nothing. We had hope. A future. We could have worked. Studied. Now there's nothing. Now I have no one.'

Agnes poured water into paper cups. They sat under the tree. Medodzi took a sip of water. '"England," my brother used to say. "On a good day, you can see it from here."' She turned to Agnes. 'Now I must go there on my own.'

The silence held their parallel thoughts. *How will you go to England? Who will you pay? How will you find the money now?*

Medodzi broke the silence. 'Them men, who come in their big cars, who make the plans, who bring the boats. They promised my brother and they broke their promise. They owe me, Sister.'

That was when Agnes had said, 'You need a place of safety.' That was when Medodzi had turned to her with her mocking smile. 'You tell me where safe is. And I'll go there.'

And now, somehow, she was here, in the darkness and the rain. Somehow she had made it. To London. But not to safety.

They owe me, Sister.

And we owe her.

* * *

That night, Agnes tried to sleep. Dreams, memories. Gunshots and chaos, torchlight strafing the choking dark. Thick tangles of red wool, a skeleton washed clean at the water's edge; a dead hand leaving trails in the sand.

* * *

It was early, not yet eight, and Agnes, hammering on the door of Julius's church, almost fell inside when he opened it.

'I can't do it,' she said. 'I promised Winifred and I can't do it.'

'What's happened? Agnes . . .' He led her inside, sat her down in a chair.

'I've hardly slept. Winifred said to leave it on the beaches, but I saw her — I really did. She seems to have managed to get to London — I don't know how, some kind of miracle. But she ran away and I can't find her. But we owe her, Julius. We owe her.'

'Agnes, dear — who?'

'Medodzi. The one I told you about. The one whose brother drowned. Somehow she's crossed the Channel. She's here. And Paula's here too. She knows the cloth house. I was only an alibi, but why did she need an excuse to visit them? And then he goes and kills himself. I've been thinking about it, why this non-disclosure stuff, as if I know something?'

Julius had been boiling the kettle, making tea, and now set a mug down in front of her, resting one hand on her shoulder.

'And your good Sister Winifred said, leave it all behind you.'

'How can I, Julius?' He waited while she took a sip of tea. 'I mean,' she went on, 'it's all very well Winifred saying that, as if it's easy, but she's not the one having to carry on normal life in the middle of—' she waved a hand towards the window — 'all this.' She looked across at him. 'Why are you smiling?'

'Was I? Oh dear,' he said. 'I just wondered what "all this" might mean.'

'Everything,' she said. 'Dead women and police tape and Frank knocking at our door, and that poor man across the road . . . and it all started with the flood, Julius, with the rain.' She stopped, breathless, took another sip of tea.

'I still don't see—'

'A tidal wave,' she said. 'It washed through the old house on the corner, it brought Celia to light, and — and Medodzi. That girl flung herself on the mercy of the waves and landed right here, in our streets, right now.'

A large gulp of tea.

Julius picked up the snowstorm from his desk, watched the scene settle in its dome. 'Agnes — it's not all the same thing, is it? I mean, that awful woman is allowed to have friends in London. And this poor man? Suicide, you say? And it may be that this girl from the camp has tracked you down, but if she needs your help she'll find you. And the lady in your cellar, with your nice chap and his tapes . . . What I mean is, it's a question of what we do about it all.'

'All what?'

'Oh, you know, human suffering, that kind of thing.' He placed the snow globe back on his desk.

Agnes took another sip. 'Quite a big question, then?'

'It's a conundrum,' he said. 'It certainly is.'

Outside, a distant church bell chimed the half hour. The early sun blinked through the trees.

Agnes placed her mug on Julius's desk. 'Athena has Nic's godson staying with them. He's a magician, Emil is.'

'He is?'

'The two of diamonds appearing on a piece of toast, that kind of thing.'

Julius raised an eyebrow. 'Now, that is magic. Almost a miracle, I'd say.'

'Don't tease, Julius.'

'Heaven knows we all need a sense of wonder in this life.'

'That's what Athena says.'

'You choose your friends wisely.'

She smiled at him.

'How are the icons?' Julius said.

'That's another thing. Sister Josephine. She's been very odd since the bones were found. And — she recognised Frank. I'm sure she did. Stared at him. And then I didn't tell her about his connection with Celia — perhaps I should have done . . .'

'No,' he said. 'It's his story. Not anyone else's.'

'But the photos — he's part of the icon collection, he must be connected to it. Why would his picture turn up with all the old catalogues? And Josephine knows the icons very well. The more I think about it, the odder it seems. She's hardly been in the library since Celia was found.'

'As I said, Agnes. There's a limit to what we can do. Gerry Nolan — I was remembering a conversation we had, out here on the steps, one day after Mass, ooh, about six, seven months ago. Last autumn, it was. Something in the news, another war, another bombing, a hospital somewhere, mothers weeping for their children . . . and after the service we were chatting, and he says to me, "The thing is, Father, these are the baby steps of the human race. These teetering, toddling steps are just the beginning. That's why we're getting it so wrong — terrible mistakes we're making, wars and killings, poisoning the oceans, trashing the planet. But we'll learn," he says to me. "We've got millennia ahead of us to get it right," he says. And I'm looking at him, and I say, "So, Gerry, what you mean is there's a future where we're benign and enlightened beings who know how to behave?" And he thought for a moment, like he hadn't considered it, and then he says, "You know what, Padre? I think I prefer us as we are."'

The sunlight filtered through the leaded window.

'I need to get back,' she said.

He looked across at her. 'Will you be okay?'

'I'll have to be. Perhaps I should just contemplate your benign future in which we do no harm.'

'You'll be here some time, then.'

She smiled.

'They'll be missing you at Lauds,' he said.

'I'll be back in time for Mass.'

'And will you do as Winifred asked?'

'I have to.' She gathered up her coat, her bag.

On the steps, he gave her a brief hug. 'The baby steps of the human race,' he said. 'One day we'll start to get the hang of it all. Just a shame I won't be here to see it.'

CHAPTER TWELVE

'How can she be there? Medodzi? She really stole a dinghy, on her own, in that storm?' Winifred's voice was loud on her phone.

It was late morning, after Mass, and Agnes sat in her room.

'And why did she run away from you?' Winifred was saying. 'I mean, to get to your convent, she must have been following you. Are you sure it was her?'

'Do you remember those rainbow trainers? She was wearing them.'

'Poor kid. She must be starving. Still, now she knows where you are, she can find you again.'

'Perhaps she was following Paula?' Agnes said, aware of the thought forming as she said it.

'Paula? Why?'

'She was angry with Paula, wasn't she? And she knew Paula was coming here to see me. And she'd have worked out where the convent is; it's easy to track down.'

'But — how on earth has she got to London? Did the coastguards rescue her? She'd still be in Dover or wherever?'

'None of it makes sense. If Paula only came to see me as an alibi to see the people down the road—'

'But then why would she hide that?'

'I keep going over it. All that confiding in me about her father, and her need to succeed. And being rude about her poor sister, who I'm sure is a much nicer person than she is.'

Winifred laughed.

'It's like Paula wanted me to confide something in her. And I've no idea what it is.'

'Well, if she comes back, like she said she would, perhaps you'll find out.'

* * *

Agnes left her room in the Sunday silence and went down the stairs to the library.

She pulled out one of the box files. She sat down beside it, rested her hand on it.

She thought about Josephine, unable to pray with those bones beneath her feet. Haunted by the ghosts of the long-dead.

And now a man from the house on the corner has shot himself. And if I was to call Sandra and say, I know this woman, she visited him, maybe it's a bigger story — and now there's a troubled young woman on the loose in London, swearing some kind of vengeance to do with her brother, and she's either followed me, or her, or both . . .

She pulled the box towards her, opened the lid.

So, Celia Danziger had stayed in this house, fallen ill and at some point in the seventies had gone into the cellar and died. She'd left no trace, perhaps because she'd used a pseudonym; and Frank's father had been heartbroken.

And guilty. Perhaps.

Making up stories, Julius would say. Like all these people who want him to tell the true story of Gerry Nolan.

The box file had pages of typewritten research, yellowed at the edges. 'Some novice years ago,' Patricia had said. 'Your sisters let her loose on all this and now we've just got more chaos, but with pencil marks in the margins . . .'

The Book of Revelation features heavily here. Agnes read the neat typescript. *The seven seals are shown at the edges of the painting, with the author of the book, known as St. John, at the centre, with his scroll . . .*

'John the Revelator,' Agnes thought. '*Who's that writin' . . .*' The scratchy, wispy notes brushed against her thoughts. '*Wrote the book of the seven seals . . .*'

She went to the photographs. There it was, the colour photograph of the missing icon, the handmaid of Our Lady, dropping her spindle of red wool at the news of the Annunciation.

Spinning our fate. Or weaving our life into warp and weft. And now interrupted, for ever, by the angel's divine intervention. A rupture in the universe that tumbles the spindle to the floor.

She sat down, pulled out her phone, scrolled to Frank's number. Her finger hovered. To ask him what? *How is your father connected to our icons and to the body in our cellar?*

As Sandra had said, it's history, not criminology. *And Frank doesn't want to know.*

* * *

The afternoon passed in solitude and spreadsheets, in the settled sunlit quiet of a Sunday afternoon. She listed the paintings, Victoriana, idylls of mansion houses, landscapes. 'How on earth did you nuns end up with all this tat? Of course there's an outside chance there's an early Constable or something, but, frankly, how on earth would anyone know, the way your Order has kept it in such a mess . . .'

Haywains and carthorses. Ladies with parasols enjoying landscaped gardens.

Agnes dutifully typed in the dates, and the painter where listed.

The door opened. Josephine stood there in the slanting light. In her long-sleeved dress, her thick sandals, her hair tied back in a loose scarf, she looked like a painting, a medieval woman living her everyday life among the sacred.

'Oh,' she said, and sat down at her place. She pulled some catalogues towards her and began to make her lists.

'You weren't at Mass,' Agnes said.

Josephine looked up, shook her head and went back to her writing.

'Shall I type those lists onto the system?' Agnes asked.

'What? If you want.'

Agnes took the written pages and went to the computer.

There was a silence. The scratch of Josephine's pen, the tapping of Agnes's computer keys.

Josephine pushed the catalogues away from her with a sigh. 'I wasn't in Mass,' she said, 'because it makes no sense to me.'

Agnes stopped typing.

'Patricia calls it mumbo jumbo,' Josephine said.

'She's not very polite about nuns,' Agnes said.

'She is very rude. But she may be right.' Josephine closed the heavy book in front of her. 'I mean, all this—' she gestured to the catalogues, the lists of paintings — 'it's about more than what we do in the Mass, isn't it?'

'Is it?'

'Yes.' Her voice was emphatic. 'I mean, what are our rituals? A commemoration of an awful death? A vague hope that it wasn't in vain?'

'I think . . .' Agnes said. 'I think the Eucharist is about more than that—' But Josephine was still speaking.

'. . . the medieval world. The women, the abbesses, the authors of these texts — they could address the wider world. They were at the heart of things. Nursing, teaching, midwifery, sheltering orphans, growing food, spinning, weaving, stitching, painting. Their work could be about everything.' Her finger was tapping against the book's hard cover. 'They knew what they were for.' Her hand went to her neck, pulled at her tied-back hair.

'Do we not know what we're for?' Agnes said.

Josephine gazed at the book in front of her. 'I would say,' she said. 'I would say, no. I don't.'

'Patricia said—'

She looked up. 'What? What did she say?'

'She said you were very knowledgeable about all this. She said you were a great asset.'

Josephine frowned. 'She did?'

'She said you must have studied this "in a previous life", as if we nuns were living out a second chance.'

Josephine didn't smile. She got up, walked the length of the long table and stopped, resting her palms on the polished surface. 'I did study it,' she said. 'Briefly. But I had to stop.' She paced again, back towards her seat, paused again. 'My mother . . . her care. There was no money. I couldn't continue. I had to go back home, to Yorkshire. Then she died.'

'So — your vocation?'

Josephine paused, weighing her words. 'My vocation, as you call it, was towards this.' She waved her hand across the books. 'I just didn't see it clearly till now.'

From along the corridor came the sound of music practice from the chapel, piano phrases, the stop-start of women's voices.

'After Mother died, I thought that's what I shall do. I became a novice, in Yorkshire. We had sheep in my first order. I knew them all. I would shear them. I spun the wool, I dyed it, wove it. I was happy. Our mother abbess, we would talk about faith. And she would reassure me, tell me that faith comes from the work. That it's all the same. She was very kind to me.'

A few faint choral notes, the chanting of a psalm.

'I painted, too. Icons. Our Lady. The Angel. The spindle of wool. And then, coming across it here, finding it was missing . . .' Her voice faltered. 'It's been difficult, you see. It's like a gap. In the collection. And in me.' Her eyes filled with tears. 'A big, big gap. A void.'

She was standing unsteadily, leaning on the table with both hands. 'When I was a novice, I made a spindle. I washed the wool, combed, carded, dyed it red. And I spun it on my little spindle. I treasured it. I have it still. But, like the handmaid in the painting, there has been a split in the order of things. It is as if it has fallen from my hands.'

She looked up, gathered her cardigan around her chest. 'I don't know what to do.'

Agnes was about to speak, but Josephine turned and left the library, her long skirt swishing at her ankles.

* * *

'My soul doth magnify the Lord, and my spirit rejoices in God my saviour . . .'

Agnes looked around the nuns gathered for vespers, the faces shaded in the candlelight. There was no sign of Josephine.

She thought about the kind mother abbess, saying to Josephine that the work was enough. She wondered what it would be like to feel that it wasn't.

'He has cast down the mighty from their thrones, he has lifted up the lowly . . .'

She thought about the void that had appeared in Josephine's life, the big, big gap. The bones beneath the chapel, the upending of the natural order of things, the rupture appearing in the universe. Celia Danziger brought to light.

She thought about Josephine's recognition of Frank. She wondered at this new crisis in Josephine's life — at the spindle of red wool dropped in shock, 'fallen from my hands'.

As the candles were blown out, Agnes thought about Medodzi and wondered how to find her.

* * *

On Monday morning, when the doorbell rang, when Agnes answered it to find DS Sandra Campbell on the doorstep, she almost hugged her.

'Thought we'd finished with you lot.' Sandra followed Agnes into the office. 'And don't offer me coffee, the last lot was undrinkable. In spite of the tea ceremony.'

'Part of our penance,' Agnes said.

'Yet another good reason to be an unbeliever.' Sandra settled into a chair.

'So,' she said, 'there was a shooting, across the way there. You'll know.'

'Yes,' Agnes said.

'Can't talk about it, but at the moment we're not looking for anyone else.'

'You were questioning his wife?'

'Routine, in these cases. Poor lady.'

'Right.'

'Who'd have thought, a crime scene in that lovely house, that parquet floor, blood and brains everywhere.'

'Mmm.'

'You'd think he'd have gone out into that enormous garden at least. Anyway, the thing is — the weapon, it was the kind the little roadmen have round here. Shouldn't be telling you, but maybe all sorts come and go here. Like, why did a city trader have a Sig Sauer nine millimetre. Them gangsters on the estate up there, it's their weapon of choice for settling a minor disagreement. But odd for this gentleman to have one. Anyway,' Sandra said, 'there was a break-in. At the house. Last night. Like someone going back for something, but the wife is definitely with her sister in Hertfordshire. Might be opportunistic as the place isn't secured, all the doors rotten with the flood. It's the richest house for miles around, but nothing seems to have been taken. I just thought I'd let you know, in your parallel life as a copper.'

'Thank you,' Agnes said. 'Also—'

'What?'

'There's a missing girl,' she said. 'I know her from our charity in Calais. She appeared, on the street. She ran away. I need — I need to find her.'

Sandra sucked her teeth. 'You need to find her?'

'I know it sounds . . .'

'Impossible. That's what it sounds. Do you have a photo?'

Agnes shook her head. 'She's wearing rainbow-coloured trainers.'

Sandra smiled. 'Well, that narrows it down. You should see my in-tray — an ever-growing mountain. Soon I won't be able to see over the top and no one will know where I am. Which might be an advantage.'

Agnes laughed.

'Text me her details. I'll put out a shout. But what I really think is, Sister, if she needs to find you, she will. She knows where you are.'

'That's what my fellow sister said.'

'All of you.' Sandra got to her feet. 'Nuns. Coppers. It's a fine line. And the coffee's better on my side, promise. Keep in touch,' she said, going to the door. 'Laters, eh?'

* * *

As Agnes was going to her room, her phone rang.

'It's Frank,' he said. 'Frank Tillman. I've been doing me some thinking.'

With one hand she opened the curtains in her room.

'Those photos,' he said. 'You told PC Plod?'

'I had to,' she said.

'It's okay. It's Celia's history, it makes no odds. But history, you see — it doesn't go away. You can't say, this is how it is here, unless you also know, this is how it was then.'

'Right.' Agnes sat on her bed.

'You've listened to the tapes. Music, you say.'

'It kind of breaks through. Gospel singing. "*God shall wipe away all tears*."'

'Odd. Doesn't ring a bell.'

'And "John the Revelator".'

'*Who's that writin'? John the Revelator.*' Frank's voice was tuneful.

93

'That's the one.'

'*Wrote the book of the seven seals.*'

'You know it,' she said.

'Yes. But I can't see what it's got to do with my father.'

'Tape breakthrough, perhaps.'

'Ah.'

There was a silence. 'You see, Sister — there's a conflict. I'm grateful, to you and your kind friend with the tape recorder. But the truth is, I have walked with a lighter step since all those old carrier bags were out of my life. It is hard won, this lightness in my spirit. I do not want to give it up. But, then, somewhere in your convent, among a collection to do with Russian iconography — a photograph of me appears. Taken by Celia, I'm sure. I remember that bicycle trip. Which means I'm entangled — if not with my father, then with her. And even if there's nothing untoward about her death, her case is on file, as your nice policewoman said. It isn't over, is it? Those biblical rains have brought her to light and with her, her story and mine. I don't know what to do.'

She watched a moth settle on the window outside. 'Frank,' she said. 'You don't have to do anything.'

'When you take holy orders,' he said. 'Does it disentangle you?'

She smiled. 'Now there's a question.'

'I mean, your parents, your childhood. Do nuns get angry?'

'It's like this,' she said. 'Holy orders, as you call them. It doesn't disentangle you. You still have to do the work. But perhaps the vows we make give us the tools to do it. If we're lucky.'

'Ah.'

'And, yes. Nuns do get angry.'

'So the tools have their limits.' She heard his smile on the phone.

'We're only human,' she said.

'I shall go now,' he said. 'My father's heavy tread is fainter. Please keep in touch. Goodbye.'

Agnes put her phone down on her desk. The music flickered in her thoughts. '*Who's that writin'? John the Revelator . . . Who's that writin' . . .*'

Entanglement, she thought. *Like a spindle thread, the wool spinning our story, round and round.*

I should have mentioned Paula to Sandra Campbell.

What does Frank know about his father that he still has to hide?

CHAPTER THIRTEEN

On Tuesday morning, Agnes was interrupted in the library. 'I'm so sorry,' Sister Birgitta said. Patricia pursed her lips and typed more furiously. Donald gave her a cheery wave. 'Someone asking for you,' Sister Birgitta said to Agnes. 'At least, I think it's you she meant. "One of you sisters," she said. "She has short hair, brown with bits of grey, a bit abrupt but kind of sympathetic. Tall." I thought she must mean you. She said you spoke to her last week.'

* * *

Stephanie was standing on the convent doorstep. Still smart, in tailored trousers, but her hair was uneven, her face unmade-up. 'I need you to see my house,' she said. 'Now.'

Agnes grabbed a jacket.

'Cursed,' Stephanie said as Agnes followed her across the street. 'That's what people say. I never liked the house and clearly it wasn't just me. A break-in,' she said, as they walked up the drive. 'But how would you know if someone has broken in, past all this, doors off the hinges . . .'

She pushed the front door closed, leaning her shoulder against it. They stood in the hallway. 'This is my house.' She gave a bleak smile, a shrug. 'At least. It was. Before—' she gestured around her — 'all this.'

The hall was wide and dimly lit, the daylight muted by the half-shuttered windows. The walls bore tidemark stains, their former tasteful cream now blotched and peeling. The parquet floor was discoloured, gapped and lifting. Stephanie glanced down at her feet and gave a small shiver. 'The lounge might be more comfortable.'

She led the way along an unlit corridor, which opened out into a large room. French windows showed the garden beyond. Paintings hung on the pale blue walls. But there was still the dank chill, and the dark blue carpet seemed thick and moist at their feet.

Stephanie flung herself into an armchair. She faced Agnes. 'I don't know what to do.'

Agnes found a dry edge of the sofa and sat down. 'It's a lovely house.'

'Perhaps. In about a hundred years it might be. But not for me.' She gave a small, polite shrug. 'How am I going to live here without him?'

'I can see that.'

'Just me and the baby. And the insurance claim, which as far as I can see is going to take me the rest of my life in emails and forms and signatures and lawyers, and all on my own, no help, no support . . .' Her voice roughened, cracked.

'Where is your baby?'

'What? Oh, with my sister.' She smoothed a hand across her forehead. 'I sound ungrateful. My sister has been a trooper. She has one of her own, a little boy.' She looked up. 'How's your . . . lady in the cellar?'

'It's been rather a challenge,' Agnes said.

'Police everywhere. Tell me about it.' The smile faded. 'The thing is . . .'

Agnes waited.

'I mean,' Stephanie went on, 'he had all sorts of reasons to kill himself and he'd talked of it before, but I never thought he'd do it. He had everything to live for. Our baby, she's adopted. We went through so much to get her — you can't know how complicated it is these days. It made our family complete. A new life to think about.' Her face clouded. 'I just keep thinking, how could he? And that method . . . a gun . . . like, where the hell did he find it?' There was a catch in her voice.

Agnes waited, then said, 'When you say he had all sorts of reasons . . . ?'

Stephanie breathed a sigh. 'Well, I can tell you this. Turns out we owe money. I feel so stupid, me working in finance. He — he borrowed for this . . .' She looked around her. 'This house. He said his father had lent him the money, but I spoke to David yesterday and he was appalled. He'd said no. "He did ask," he told me. "And I told him to stand on his own two bloody feet."' Her eyes welled with tears. 'He's quite a nice man, actually — I don't want to give the wrong impression. But . . . Adam always thought he was a failure. Whatever he did wasn't good enough for his dad. And I think with his father refusing him money, there'd have been a huge row; it would have festered . . .'

'But,' Agnes said, 'the night he died . . .'

'Well, yes. Why then? That's what I've been asking myself.'

'Paula was here.'

'Yes. They talked. Shut away in the study. Maybe he was trying to borrow from her? I keep thinking, why didn't he tell me, why didn't he leave a note . . . but then I think, that would be worse, wouldn't it? You'd really think you'd let them down, if you could read their last words.' She dashed tears from her eyes. 'And then the police have said that weird thing, that they haven't ruled anything out, like it might not be suicide. Apparently the gun he used, it's used a lot round here in drug-dealing feuds. No one can work out where he got it from. Least of all me.' She straightened up, leaned back in the chair. 'But who on earth would want him dead? A robbery, I asked them? A random attack? I think they know he did it, but they're waiting to be sure.'

She reached into a pocket for a tissue, dabbed at her eyes. 'Oh God. It's like I'm waiting to wake up. All this . . .' She gestured at the room, the furniture pulled away from the walls, the carpet curling at the edges. 'If he did get into debt . . . it's because he wanted us to be happy. He always wanted things to be perfect. He thought you could buy happiness.' She began to cry again. 'Sister, I don't know what I'm going to do.'

She gave a ragged sob, then jumped to her feet suddenly. 'Come upstairs.'

Agnes followed her up the wide staircase and onto the generous landing, the banisters of polished mahogany untouched by the flood.

The rooms were lighter, the curtains drawn open, the sense of damp diminished.

'The nursery,' Stephanie said. There was pink wallpaper, with elephants, lions, koala bears. A child's bed, stripped bare. 'I had to rescue all the bed linen.'

The wardrobe was flung open; the chest of drawers had been emptied. Children's toys were scattered across the floor.

'Police,' Stephanie said. 'Or the burglars. Both of them, turning my house upside down.' She gazed around the room. 'I wish they'd tell me what's going on.'

Agnes looked at Stephanie, standing alone amid the teddies, the books, the bright bricks of pink and blue. 'If it was suicide . . .'

Stephanie shook her head. 'It makes no sense. He had everything to live for, our child — he loves her so much, she changed his life. He grew up so differently, you see, and with me, and this house, and his business . . . he'd made the life he wanted. And then our accountant told me about the gap in his finances. But Benjamin's mystified too, said it wasn't insurmountable. What I think is, it was his huge sense of failure. He wanted the perfect life for me, for our family. If he felt he'd let us down, that might have pushed him over the edge . . .'

She turned away, led them out of the nursery. 'You see, he was an only child, his father was in the military, high up.

They lived everywhere, the Far East, Egypt . . . but don't get him started on Woking. That was the family home — just him and his mum half the time, a local school, a sense that life was happening elsewhere. And they weren't well off, that's the myth about army officers. Adam wanted to put something right. To be the kind of man his father wanted him to be. And he was bloody well going to make it with us . . .'

They stood on the landing. There was sunlight through the arched window, a glitter of dust in its beams.

'And his business?' Agnes asked.

'He got himself to Cambridge, entirely on his own hard work.' She gave a brief smile. 'There's me with my ponies and ballet and home counties school for girls. My mother was worried I wouldn't be clever enough for him. He did natural sciences — I think that's what they called it. Went into the City. And then all this green-economy stuff, became something of an expert. Not just money, you see. Making the world a better place too.'

'And Paula?'

'Oh, her.' Again, the polite shrug. 'She would use the same language. But I don't think she wants to make the world a better place. Just better for her. She's Adam's friend really, not mine. They met at Cambridge. After college they went into a start-up — management consultancy — but then Adam went into banking. Paula stayed more in the corporate world. Her last job went a bit wrong, Adam said, and then she went into the charity sector, still on the finance side, as you know. I never thought she was that keen on refugees. And now with this job offer last week, headhunted, she said. Big international think tank, based in Canary Wharf — as she said, "It's not as if working for a scuzzy little charity is ever going to give you a damehood."' She gave a small laugh. 'Oh dear, how rude of me, but that's what she's like. I said to her, "But it's not scuzzy — it really matters to help those poor people who've ended up there. They need a life, don't they? They need a future." But she just gave that funny smile she has, you know, kind of like she knows something you don't.'

Agnes remembered.

'Adam said she was the most ambitious person he knew.'

'A job offer?'

Stephanie nodded. 'That's what Adam said, after she'd gone.'

'Were she and Adam close?'

She gave an uneasy smile. 'I think she had hopes of him at one point. But she's not his type. He once said, marriage to Paula would be a kind of serfdom. And he's someone who liked her. The thing is . . .' She brushed dust from the window-sill with the palm of her hand. 'They were deep in conversation the night before he died. Shut themselves away for quite a while. Adam was cross afterwards. "She thinks I owe her." I got the feeling she wanted him to pull strings for this new job. His old school friend, Chris, is quite high up there, it's a small world. Maybe she was worried that whatever had gone wrong in that previous company might cloud things with this new job interview.' She leaned against the landing wall. 'Adam told me afterwards that he'd tried to explain that wasn't how those things worked. That it might backfire. Also, he said, Paula's going to get what she wants just by being Paula, and I think that's true. She'll be fine. But he was edgy then. And he said she was really cross. And then she went off to her hotel.'

'How did you and Adam meet?'

She drew a curtain back, letting in a shaft of sunlight. 'In a coffee shop in Cannon Street. Cliché, I know. A glance over the oat milk latte. I was working for a fund, you won't have heard of it, based in Zurich half the time. Really fun, I loved it. And there he was, in his suit and tie and loafers. And we got talking, something about US bonds and futures in wheat, I don't know . . .' The smile faded. She tapped a foot against the landing carpet, smoothed an edge. 'It was a world I loved. People get the wrong idea about the City. Half the time we're just making sure people get the pensions they've worked so hard for.'

She took a step towards the staircase. 'Of course, I had to give up work with the baby. But Adam was determined to

create the family he'd never had. The perfect life. All this . . .'
She led them back down the stairs.

They were back in the dim, dank hallway.

'He set his heart on this house. It's not even beautiful. My mother when she saw it, went on about nouveau riche Victorians in unfashionable parts of London. I think he liked it because it's bigger than any of the others.'

'And it survived the Blitz,' Agnes added. 'Like our convent.'

'He'd go on about being a Londoner, how our daughter will be a Londoner too . . . I always thought it was because he didn't know where he belonged.'

'Not Woking, then.'

She shook her head. 'He needed to create a history. This house gave that to him. Whereas me . . .' She managed a smile. 'We Chesneys have been in our village for ever. My parents lived and died there, that's where my sister is too.'

She drew her phone out of her bag, glanced at it. 'Talking of which, I'd better get back. Amy's been on child duty since this morning.'

Outside, she locked the front door carefully. 'No point, really. The flood's wrecked all the door frames, so anyone can get in. Police are going through CCTV, but what's that going to tell them?'

Her heels crunched along the gravel drive.

'Thank you for being there,' Stephanie said, out in the street. 'It was nice to talk to you.' She brushed her hair away from her face. Her expression was empty. 'I don't know what I'm going to do,' she said. She hesitated. 'Well. My car's just here. Back on the A10, I suppose. I'd put music on to pass the time, but nothing helps. Nothing.' Her voice cracked. She turned away, murmuring goodbyes.

* * *

'And I bet however sorry you felt for her, kitten, you envied her the car.'

'An Audi Q5e. Hybrid, you know.' Agnes held the phone to her ear above the noise of the high street. 'I just thought, the A10 couldn't be that bad in a car like that.'

'Poor cow, though,' Athena said. 'All that to deal with. Still, at least she's got her little girl. That must be some consolation. Better go, sweetie, someone at the door. Maybe a customer prepared to carry away a bundle of fishnets. Or fishing nets. Either would suit me. Lunch soon — I'll message you.'

* * *

Agnes let herself into the convent, went straight to the office.

Athena's right — I shouldn't envy Stephanie her car.

Wireless charging pad. Memory seats. Heads-up dashboard display.

She sat at the office desk.

Perhaps I could persuade the Order that we need to upgrade from the Polo.

CHAPTER FOURTEEN

Agnes closed down the Audi website and stared at the screen. She clicked the mouse, typed in two names.

Paula Gerrard. Adam Crosland.

Where to start?

She clicked on Adam's name. Almost immediately there he was, fresh-faced and smart in a gallery of similarly keen and smiling people. *Our Team*, it said.

She read his brief biography. *Cambridge. Natural Sciences. Interest in Climate Economics . . .*

Still present tense. No update yet. Still in this world.

Paula Gerrard. Again, almost instantly, there she was, CEO, overseeing a group of charities of which the Order's work in France was one. Scuzzy or not, Agnes thought, as she read the glowing biographical paragraph, all the roles that had led to her inexorable rise. And now, apparently, headhunted for a new job in London.

She could hear Patricia's voice in the corridor, being forceful about deadlines — 'need for urgency . . . hopelessly under-staffed . . .' — and Sister Christiane's softer, measured replies.

She went back to the screen.

Companies House.

Names of Directors.

She typed in Adam's name. Scrolled down.

There they both were. Adam and Paula. The name of a company. Both directors. Company dissolved years ago. So, that was the start-up they'd gone into all that time ago. Just as Stephanie had said.

Old friends, met at university. An interest in finance and climate science. And money.

Why shouldn't Paula visit him? The night before her job interview.

The night before he chose to die.

Patricia's voice, still grumbling, faded towards the stairs. Agnes logged off and went to the library.

* * *

There were new plastic crates, with the beginnings of piles of leather-bound catalogues stacked in them.

'Where is she?' Patricia barked as Agnes appeared.

'Who?'

'Your sister. Josephine, of course. This was her task and she's buggered off.'

'I'm sorry . . . I don't know . . . She wasn't at lunch.' Agnes sat at the laptop.

Patricia came and sat next to her, breathing heavily. 'Sister,' she said. 'I think she's stolen it. I told Donald, and he said, "Ask that other one, the clever one." So I am.'

Agnes pushed the laptop away. 'I don't understand.'

'Your fellow Sister Josephine. That icon, the Annunciation. The Angel and the Virgin Mary. It was definitely here. If you follow the catalogues, it was with the other two. Each year, it appears in the lists. So — where is it? A thing like that doesn't just get lost.'

Agnes turned to face her. 'Why do you think it was Josephine?'

Patricia's voice was a loud whisper. 'Don't you think she's been behaving oddly? I mean, I know you all do, but her more than most.'

Agnes realised she hadn't seen Josephine since their talk on Sunday night.

'And,' Patricia went on, 'she's obsessed with that photo. You know, the colour plate. Such a wonderful example. But the other day she said to me, "Don't go telling people it's a portrait. Because it isn't." An odd thing to say, don't you think? I mean, I have to concede the point — she does seem to have a great expertise in all this. Really most impressive. And her grasp of Russian is enviable.'

'Patricia,' Agnes said, 'why would she steal it? It's priceless. She must know it's serious theft. And it's not as if she can do anything with it.'

'To keep, I suppose. If she loves it that much. The other day she reprimanded me again. "Devotional objects," she said. "That's what these are. Never lose sight of that." And look—' Patricia reached for a catalogue on Agnes's desk — 'this entry here . . .' She flicked through the pages with her ringed fingers. 'She's underlined it. That's definitely her, she was reading through this two days ago and no one else has looked at it.'

Agnes followed the pointed finger to the printed text.

. . . *the Annunciation. In this icon, the Angel Gabriel appears to the Virgin Mary. Dated about 1450. The handmaid of the Virgin stands behind her holding a spindle of red wool, which she has dropped in shock. The icon is one of several depicting the schism in the fate of humanity, the redemption of our Fall through the Immaculate Conception, the coming of God himself into the world.*

'See.' Patricia pointed again. 'She's underlined "a spindle of red wool" and "the schism in the fate of humanity" — that redemption bit.'

'Patricia,' Agnes said, 'what do you want me to do?'

'Get the bloody thing back, that's what. Who'd have thought you nuns would all be so temperamental — ah, here's Donald.'

Donald came into the room carrying a large brown paper carrier bag. 'Lunch,' he said. 'Roquefort cheese. And celeriac remoulade. And I got some decent sourdough from those women at that bakery who know what they're doing . . .' He glanced at Agnes, at Patricia still sitting at a conspiratorial angle. 'She's told you her theory, then?'

'I certainly have, Donald. Sister Agnes has promised to help.'

Donald flicked a glance at Agnes. 'We all do as we're told, don't we?'

'You can laugh, Donald, but it's serious. The Order specifically called on us because they know we're expert and we can be trusted to sell on their behalf. So, here we are, tasked with all this cataloguing, valuing and sorting, and yet constantly thwarted by light-fingered members of their community.' She threw a corner of turquoise silk scarf over one shoulder. 'I mean, we didn't even have this problem when they closed down that old jail in Plymouth, do you remember, and they called us in? An exquisite Pre-Raphaelite collection, long forgotten, all hidden away in their attics from when the building had been a private house, and the inmates couldn't have been more helpful. I don't remember any of those lovely old lifers hiding away the odd Rossetti under their prison-issue jackets.'

Donald was taking a loaf of bread out of the paper bag and now began to laugh.

'I don't see what's so funny,' Patricia said.

'No, dear. It isn't funny at all.' He began to laugh again.

'I mean, if that icon really has gone missing . . .'

'Quite.' He put out plates, brandished a bread knife.

'Donald, dear, you can't possibly be intending to eat lunch so near the collection.'

'No, dear. Of course not. I thought I'd go over to those empty desks there.' He began to laugh again.

'Now what's funny?' She stood up, one hand on a hip, facing them both.

'Nothing, dear. I just think Sister Agnes here is amused by the idea of prison-issue jackets.'

Agnes smiled. 'It would solve the problem of what kind of habit to wear in the twenty-first century.'

'And terribly practical.'

'Oh, honestly, Donald. Anyway, Agnes has agreed to help track down the missing item.'

'Well, if anyone can find it, she can.' He turned to her with a smile. 'Would you like to share our Roquefort?'

'She's had lunch,' Patricia said.

* * *

Late that evening, Agnes sat in her room with the Order's laptop. Staring, once again, at the two names in the old Companies House entry.

On her desk lay the printed-out documents that Paula wanted her to sign.

She skimmed through the clauses of the agreement, seeing only empty promises in contractual prose.

An alibi, Winifred had said.

Or a pretext?

Our convent right by the old sailcloth house.

That's why she came to see me. She doesn't need these papers. My signature means nothing at all.

So, she'd come back to this part of town. A job interview. And — Adam. Closeted together. And then, Adam was cross. If Adam had financial problems . . . did he owe her?

If Adam didn't kill himself . . . ?

Agnes shut down the laptop.

A mad idea. Only the thinking of a temperamental nun.

She flicked through the NDA papers again. *Paula thinks I know something. But what? What happened, when she suddenly told me I was no longer needed at the centre? What did she think I'd found out?*

Agnes stared out at the London night. She thought about the drowning. Was that what had started it? They'd all been traumatised, it's true. Having to bury him, in the rain, his sister weeping for the life he might have led. But then some weeks had passed and things had calmed down. Agnes had moved from the kitchen rota to the office — it had been calmer there — organising food orders on the phone, taking messages. Paula's idea. 'They can use the landline, these people, if they want to speak to me. I'm not giving out my mobile number to the pen-pushers of the French state . . .'

They'd been reduced to Post-it notes, slips of paper snatched by Paula and left unread, tucked impatiently under a large crystal paperweight that had sat on her desk. 'These people, don't they know I'm busy . . . ?'

That had been Agnes's last, uncontroversial role. A few weeks of filing and phone messages — and then the meeting. 'I'm so sorry, Agnes, but we need to shift things around a bit. I know you took that drowning to heart, and we all feel it would be better for you to be back in the peace and quiet of your convent . . .'

What had changed? What happened?

What do I know, that I don't know, that she thinks I know?

Her phone rang.

Frank. His voice was shaky. 'I need to hear those tapes. Whatever it is he's going on about. I need to hear it.'

'But—'

'I've found more. It's all changed. Can I meet you both, you and your nice priest friend?'

CHAPTER FIFTEEN

Julius watched the snow settle on Tower Bridge. He put the snow globe down on his desk and looked up.

'What do you think he wants to tell us?'

'Julius, I've no idea. He just said it had all changed.'

'It's after four now. Do you think he'll come?'

As he spoke, they heard the bell chime from the church side door. Agnes jumped up.

A moment later she led Frank into Julius's office.

'Ah,' Frank said. 'You must be—'

Julius got to his feet. 'Father Julius.' He held out his hand.

'You've rescued us, I gather,' Frank said. 'Technology, all that.' Frank was wearing an aged dark-grey raincoat, damp from the afternoon drizzle, and was carrying a small brown leather case.

'Yes.' Julius pointed to the tape machine that was sitting on a side table by his desk.

Agnes pulled up a wooden chair next to hers, found a cushion. Frank sat down heavily. 'Thank you,' he said. 'For allowing me this. I thought I could leave it all behind, but, of course, it's impossible. A man like my father . . . He was determined to make his mark.' He placed the case on his lap and unzipped it. 'This is why I'm here. Look.'

It was a letter, typewritten on yellowing paper.

'I found it yesterday, in between the pages of this book. One of his Russian things. I was packing them up for the charity shop, and I opened this book, and this letter fell out.'

He placed it on the desk, smoothing it with both hands. 'From a doctor. A GP. In answer, clearly, to one of his. Look.'

Agnes picked it up. She read the neat typescript.

Dear Professor Tillman,

I am writing in reply to your letter of the fifth of June. I have discussed your position with my colleagues here. We are all, of course, sympathetic to your view and we are touched by your concern for Miss Danziger. As physicians, we do understand the severity of her illness. However, we cannot possibly admit her apparent wish to die as evidence in your support. We urge you to put all such ideas to one side and to continue instead in your caring duties insofar as is possible.

There was an illegible signature and the name of a doctor underneath.

Agnes passed the letter to Julius.

She turned to Frank. 'What does that mean?'

He shook his head. 'I don't know, but it doesn't sound good, does it?'

'He — he was going to help her to die?'

Frank adjusted his weight on the rickety chair. 'I think — I think I'd better listen to the tape. If you don't mind.'

Julius folded the letter in two and handed it back to Frank. He stood up. He placed the tape on the machine, wound it on a bit, pressed play.

'. . . I will never understand why she left. Not a day goes by when I don't ache with longing for her. There. I can say it out loud, alone here, with just you, my whirring witness, at my side. I miss her. And as the weeks go by, as they lengthen

into months, I fear the worst. For some time I imagined her happy and carefree, living a new life elsewhere, a sunny shore, a cocktail in her hand . . . but now, as the silence thickens with no word from her at all, I fear that she lies dead and cold, and that I will never see her again . . .'

Again, the silence, the clunk, the crackle. Julius pressed stop.

Frank was motionless, his eyes fixed on the machine. He waved towards it. 'Go on.'

Julius wound forward, pressed play. They heard the faded piano, the rustle of the female singing voice. 'No,' Frank said. 'More . . .'

A click. A winding on.

'It is a source of some amazement to me, after all these years, that my feelings are the same. I am so different to the man I was then, and yet the mystery is, that the yearning, the love that I feel for her, is just the same. Unchanged. In some way it is a consolation . . .'

The voice stopped. Just the pulse of the tape, the whirr of the spool. Then once again there was the singing, clearer now. '*God shall wipe away all tears,*' the voice sang. '*All tears from their eyes . . .*' The voice faded into broken notes, then silence.

Julius switched off the machine.

Frank brought out a large white handkerchief and dabbed at his eyes. 'His bloody whirring bloody witness . . .' He stuffed the handkerchief back into his top pocket. 'I've never known a man so private, so ring-fenced, so . . .' His voice failed. He shook his head. 'Withholding,' he said. 'From his own bloody son. I had patients in my clinic damaged by the same thing. All the time. These men . . .' He pointed at the tape player. 'These men who are incapable of love. He denied my mother. He denied me. And then he decides he loves someone who becomes — who becomes a figment of his imagination. That's all she ever was to him in the end.

That's how he can believe himself in love with her. And even then.' His voice was loud now. 'Even then he wants to kill her.'

They sat, held by the noisy silence of the London afternoon.

Julius was studying the book. It had a red-leather cover, and thick yellowing pages printed in Cyrillic.

'Your patients . . .' Agnes said.

Frank lifted his head. 'Psychologist,' he said. 'Used to be. NHS. Retired early.'

'Ah,' she said.

He picked up the tape box, looked at the dusty cardboard. 'I never could do them justice, my patients,' he said. 'In that work . . . you glimpse the damage underneath. You want to say, "Find a psychotherapist, someone who will sit with you on this long, long journey upon which you must embark." What could I do? We were parcelled out, thinly, to work with groups, in workplaces, patching people up, making them function as best they could.'

'You could have trained,' Julius said. 'As a therapist?'

A vehement shake of his head. 'And then what? Years of my own long, long journey? Picking away at this.' He tapped the tape box. 'And finding only silence. No,' he said. 'I decided to weave my own story. Leave behind my father's disappointment, his belief that he was wronged by life.'

'And did that work?' Julius said.

Frank smiled at him. 'As well as anything else, I guess. I read. I listen to music. Chopin. Ravel. I play the piano, badly. I grow vegetables. Also badly. The sweetcorn was eaten by mice this year.'

'That was hardly your fault,' Julius said.

'No,' Frank agreed. 'Sometimes one can blame the mice.' He placed the box on Julius's desk. 'Who is the voice, the singing?'

Agnes shrugged. 'We've no idea.'

'Me neither,' Frank said. 'No idea at all.'

'He might have reused a tape,' Julius said.

'*God shall wipe away all tears,*' Frank said. 'Is that what you people think?' He held up his hand as Julius was about to speak. 'Don't tell me,' he said. 'You'll say it's a long answer.'

Julius smiled. 'Exactly that.'

Frank began to button his raincoat.

Agnes turned to him. 'What do you want us to do?'

He picked up the letter. 'What I think we should do is show this letter to the police.' He handed it to Agnes.

'Are you sure?' Agnes said.

'Yes. Then my father's life can be a matter for the state. And I can be rid of it.' He got to his feet.

Agnes stood up too. 'Even if . . .'

'Even if he's implicated in the death of your lady in the cellar?' Frank straightened his coat, tied his belt. 'I'd rather the police puzzled over it. Then I don't have to. PC Plod can have the book as well, I'm sure the Met are fluent in Russian these days.'

Julius led the way towards the door. Frank held out his hand. 'It's good to meet you,' he said to him. 'I can see why she relies on you.' A nod of his head towards Agnes, a smile to them both. Then he stepped out into the gloom of the afternoon.

Julius closed the door. He went to the tape machine, wound the spool back, placed the tape in its cardboard box.

'Well,' he said.

Agnes was sitting by his desk.

He came and sat opposite. He picked up the snow globe and studied it. 'Did his father kill that woman?'

Agnes looked at him.

'I mean,' he went on, giving the globe a shake, watching the snow settle, 'I know it's more the sort of thing you'd ask rather than me, but . . . in this case . . . I can see what you mean about your shivery feeling.'

Agnes breathed a sigh. 'Celia was dying. Frank's father wanted to help her? Some kind of assisted dying, perhaps, asking that doctor for medication? And she died anyway,' Agnes went on. 'In our cellar. Which was then a house full of old lefties and vegetarians, according to Patricia.'

He smiled.

'What shall we do?' she asked.

He put the globe on his desk. 'We do as he asks. We tell your nice policewoman.'

'Okay.' Agnes folded the letter into the book and put them both into her bag.

Julius got to his feet, glanced outside at the darkness. 'Look,' he said. 'She's there.'

Agnes could see, bent beneath a tree in his churchyard, a woman with a little girl.

'The seedlings are coming up; I've seen them,' he said. 'And at least she smiles at me now.'

* * *

When Agnes got off the bus in Hackney, she had the sense of being followed.

CHAPTER SIXTEEN

Agnes woke before the dawn. A soft chime from her alarm reminded her it was her turn to light the chapel candles. She rose, dressed, passed silently along the convent corridor.

The chapel was dark, pillared, shadowed.

There was a figure kneeling in the pews. Long skirts, headscarf. Pale face resting in prayer.

Agnes went and sat near her.

Josephine turned briefly. 'Ah,' she whispered. 'You.'

Neither of them moved. Then Agnes said, 'The woman in the cellar.'

Josephine stared straight ahead. 'Sister, I don't know anything.'

'Something is weighing heavily,' Agnes said.

Josephine flinched. 'Sometimes,' she whispered. 'Sometimes I can hardly breathe.'

Agnes's voice was low in the chapel's darkness. 'There's a man, Mr. Tillman, he came to see us. About the woman. You seemed to recognise him.'

'What?' The whisper had become a sharp out-breath. 'What are you saying, Sister?'

Josephine turned to face her. Agnes saw she was holding a book, a red-leather-bound volume.

'Frank Tillman,' Agnes said.

Josephine lifted herself from a kneeling position, breathing heavily. She sat down on a pew. 'Frank,' she said. 'His son.' She looked at the book in her hands, as if it would provide some kind of answer.

'You knew him? Mr. Tillman?'

'Professor Tillman. I studied in a class he taught. Russian.'

'Did you know Celia Danziger?'

'No.' She snapped the book shut. 'No, I didn't.' She tucked the book into her pocket.

'Josephine,' Agnes said. 'The missing icon . . .'

'It will be time to light the candles soon,' Josephine said. Her voice was unsteady, her gaze fixed on the altar — the simple wooden cross, the purple cloth, the white walls beyond.

Agnes took a deep breath. 'Patricia is worried that—'

Josephine crunched her skirt into fistfuls. 'That I've stolen it? Typical of her. Typical of her to get you to do her dirty work too. She could bloody well ask me herself. It's only because she knows its value and she wants to sell it. Well, she's wrong — it's not for sale. No one is going to put a price on it. It's beyond value. It's the truth, that's all. Our Lady as the redemption of our Fall, because of the baby she's carrying. And the red wool, that's about the cord that ties us to our mother, to life itself, the cord that's severed on our death. That's why the maid drops it, because we have eternal life now, through the Mother of God. It's the pulling apart of the fabric of the universe, a revolution in the order of things . . .' She was breathing fast, her eyes darting. She jumped to her feet. 'You can tell all that to your friend Patricia too.'

She hurried from the pew, ran from the chapel.

At breakfast she was nowhere to be seen.

* * *

The archive was in chaos. Boxes had been brought out, lids removed, papers stacked in heaps on the desks.

'Only thing for it, Agnes,' Patricia said. 'We're running out of time. Our instructions were clear — to sort everything out, list everything for the valuation and sell anything you no longer wish to store.'

Agnes looked at a newly stacked crate.

'That,' Patricia said. 'Victoriana. Load of tat, but we'll take it off your hands.'

Agnes lifted a painting from the crate. It was in oil, a dark interior, a man, two women. 'It's Christ at the home of Martha and Mary,' she said. 'From St. Luke's Gospel.'

Patricia glanced across at her. 'Yes, I saw. Pretending to be Velázquez. A copy, late-nineteenth century. Pretty though — nice still-life with that gilthead bream.'

'Typical of my wife,' Donald said. 'To only see the food.'

'Martha is in the kitchen,' Agnes said. 'While Mary listens to Christ's teachings.'

'There's a lesson in there somewhere,' Donald said. 'Which I'm sure you sisters know.'

'The idea is that Mary is able to hear the eternal truth while her sister is distracted, worrying about worldly needs.'

'It's a very nice lunch she's making,' Patricia said. 'They ought to be grateful, those people listening to Jesus. Anyway, it's only a copy, and not a very good one at that.' She took the painting from Agnes and placed it back into the crate.

Donald looked up from his computer screen. 'Best to check, Sister. My wife is known for squirrelling away masterpieces here and there.'

'And you're no help, Donald.'

'Do you remember that Turner we ended up with from that crumbling pile in Norfolk?'

'We did them a favour, Donald. As well you know.'

Agnes bent to the crate and retrieved a leather-bound book. '*The Cloud of Unknowing*,' she said. 'We do kind of rely on this stuff, us nuns.'

Donald smiled. 'You'll be aware by now that my wife prefers Knowing to Unknowing.'

Agnes returned his smile.

'Just as well one of us does, Donald.'

'So true, my dear. So true.' He took the book from Agnes, turned the pages in his hands. 'But then,' he went on, 'my dear wife doesn't have to put in the work like you nuns do.'

'Donald, what are you going on about?' Patricia turned over a page in her file, scribbled a note in a margin.

'I'm just pointing out that Agnes here might need a medieval monastic guide from time to time. As indeed would we all, if only we'd bother to listen.'

Patricia gave a harrumph and placed the papers in a crate. 'And that's another thing,' she said. 'Any sign of your fellow sister?'

'No,' Agnes lied. 'I fear she isn't very well. I'll ask Sister Christiane later.'

'They should find us someone else. You can't do all this on your own.'

'She's a clever chap, that sister,' Donald said. 'I like her. But one does feel for her. Clearly having some kind of crisis.'

Patricia peered at him. 'Donald . . .'

'Well, I'm right, aren't I, Agnes?' He looked warm and concerned, and Agnes was reminded of Julius.

She hesitated. 'Yes.'

'Must happen a lot,' he went on. 'The challenges of your life here.' He picked up the book again. 'All this not knowing. And yet having to have faith that it all might just be true.'

Agnes smiled at him. 'Well, yes.'

'My dear wife calls it being temperamental, but as far as I can see you people are no more temperamental than the rest of us. I mean, we all have to believe in all kinds of versions of events just to keep the show on the road.'

Patricia busied herself with the books. 'Oh, he's off again. You and your theories.'

'Well, it's true, isn't it, dear? I mean, you're hardly a model of self-effacement. And I wouldn't love you nearly so much if you were.'

Patricia tutted, smiled.

'Anyway,' he said, 'how can we help your poor sister?'

'Give her a job.' Patricia faced them both. 'That's what we should do.'

Donald raised an eyebrow.

'I mean it, Donald. This next job with those old Russians in Liège — the private collection. Josephine knows more about this stuff than either of us put together. She'd be invaluable.'

'Praise indeed.' Another wink from Donald, a twinkly smile.

'I mean, obviously,' Patricia went on. 'Theft of priceless objects is a bit tricky. But if she comes to her senses, there's a job waiting for her.'

'Pat, dear, there's nothing to say she's got the bloody thing.'

'Hmm.'

'It's St. Anthony,' Donald said. 'He's the one you pray to to find missing things, isn't he, Agnes? I think we should give it a go.'

'Oh, do shut up, Donald, dear,' Patricia said, and they both laughed.

* * *

The library grew warm in the spring sunshine, the light pouring through the tall windows. Patricia's tapping on the computer seemed loud. Donald carried boxes here and there, breathing heavily, and Patricia would stop typing, look up and tut. As the morning wore on, the sunlight was obscured by clouds and the air grew heavy.

Birgitta appeared in the doorway, her sweet equanimity shadowed with a small frown.

Agnes followed her into the office.

Birgitta sat at the desk. 'I didn't know who to ask.' She looked up, a hint of unease in her blue-grey eyes. 'They need a shift at the hostel this evening. Sister Christiane is insisting I go.'

You? Agnes wanted to say, but said nothing.

'There was some kind of stand-off,' Birgitta began to explain in her clipped, gentle accent. 'A girl,' she said. 'And local people, men, angry, lots of shouting . . . Sister Dominique says it's all calmed down now, but she has a medical appointment this evening and so they need one of us there while she's gone. And — the men might come back.' Her expression clouded. 'I know we have to do as we're told, but I'm in the middle of that new altar cloth for Easter and I was going to spend the evening sewing. And I thought, perhaps, you might, as you know the place—'

'Yes,' Agnes said.

'The problem is it's obedience, isn't it? We're not supposed to make decisions about what we want. And if I tell Sister Christiane that I'd rather do the altar cloth, she'll just say that we're here to do the Lord's work.'

Agnes shifted slightly on the office chair.

Birgitta spoke again. 'When I was with the Benedictines, we could spend all day in prayer. Well, not quite . . . bits of gardening . . . mostly potatoes — I don't know what else we ate really, up in Lincolnshire — and rhubarb. The question of who we are, what we're for . . . just praising God and loving Jesus, and praying for the world. It's a balance, isn't it? Either you're enclosed or you're out in the world. I'm not sure which is right.'

'Martha and Mary,' Agnes said. 'The painting in our library. Patricia was trying to take it away. It's the two sisters in the Gospel story, when Jesus visits. One is in the kitchen cooking, the other is sitting at his feet allowing the teachings to be heard.'

'Mary's supposed to be the wiser choice,' Birgitta said. 'The idea that her concern is with the eternal truth rather than the day-to-day. That's what I was taught, anyway.'

'And then what? They'd have all been sitting there for ever, waiting for their lunch,' Agnes said, with feeling. 'Patricia was going on about the food and I do think she has a point.'

Birgitta laughed.

'My view,' Agnes said, realising she hadn't had to put it into words for a long time, 'is that we are walking alongside the presence of God. All the time. We need the contemplatives, the enclosed sisters. I'm glad they're there, praying for the world. And the world needs it more than ever. But I also think God is about doing and not just being. What I mean is, the religious life is both Martha and Mary. It needs both.'

'And you chose this?'

Agnes hesitated. 'It's a long story, where my choice to be a nun is concerned.' She took a breath. 'So — the hostel?'

'Dominique said the GP could see her this evening. Just a routine thing.'

Some trouble with a girl and some angry men. 'I'll talk to Sister Christiane,' she said. 'We do need that altar cloth. Easter is nearly upon us.'

Birgitta's face lightened. 'Thank you, Sister.'

'And while I think of it, I must get that painting chained down before Patricia tucks it under her arm.'

* * *

Christiane looked at Agnes with a sharp, narrowed gaze. Her eyes were steely grey, like her hair.

She was sitting at the desk in her room, her legs placed squarely in their thick brown sandals as she gestured to Agnes to sit down.

'Well now, Agnes.' She sank deeper into her chair, touching her hands together as if about to begin a story. 'When I was a novice, we were given tasks to which we were unequal. It was part of our training, not to attach to any personal abilities. Not to have pride. I was tasked with the floral arrangements for the chapel. It was, as you can imagine, a disaster. Old Sister Ruth would bring in a few sticks of greenery and the odd bunch of donated carnations, and in half an hour would have a marvellous pedestal, all balanced in shape and colour, that would be declared by our reverend mother as the delight of Our Lady. And mine — I mean, if you'd given me the run of the Lost Gardens of Heligan I'd have still produced a lopsided, wilting thing that was certainly not going to delight anyone at all. I know Our Lady is famed for her good manners, but it would have been a stretch even for her.'

Agnes smiled. 'And did it work?'

'Work?' Christiane looked baffled. 'Oh, I see. The sin of pride. Who knows? Would I be worse without that mortification? Probably.' She placed her hands on her lap. 'I still remember the remarks of a visiting bishop about how bold it was of our community to use the opportunity of floral display as a meditation on our inevitable decay.'

There was a twitch of a smile.

'I gather,' she went on, after a while, 'that there was some kind of fisticuffs at the hostel last night.'

Agnes nodded.

'Some poor girl having to find out that beneath all that appealing swagger was just a no-good boyo after all.'

Agnes wondered what Dominique had been saying.

'Well . . .' Sister Christiane stretched out her feet in front of her, surveyed her toes between the hefty brown straps. 'I may have faced many challenges by choosing this life, Sister, but at least I have swerved that one. For now, anyway. And—' again, that appraising asymmetrical look — 'I do agree with you, that we are running out of time for that altar cloth.' She tapped Agnes on the knee. 'Be off with you. Sister Dominique will be pleased to have your company. But I want you back in the library tomorrow morning.'

'Yes, Sister. Thank you.' Agnes got to her feet, gave a small bow and left.

* * *

The afternoon had grown heavy with impending rain, in spite of the heat. Agnes walked to the main road to catch the 388 bus to London Bridge.

Footsteps, again. She whirled, expecting to see what? Who? A lost young woman? A survivor from a Channel dinghy?

The street behind her was empty.

Why? She walked quickly. *Why do I think I'm being followed?*

Guilt, perhaps.

We let her down.

And yet . . .

Paula is in London. Winifred thinks Medodzi was heading here too.

* * *

On the bus she looked out of the window, at the coffee shops, the barbers, the stores selling groceries, vapes, household goods. She thought about Birgitta growing potatoes with the Benedictines. She thought about her own religious path that had led her here, to a seat on a bus on the Bethnal Green Road, with this smell of fried chicken and woodsmoke. She thought about Mary and Martha, and wondered whether first-century Nazareth had smelled the same.

Though maybe fish rather than chicken, she thought, sniffing the air. And no diesel. Or weed.

* * *

She walked from London Bridge towards the hostel. She turned the corner, past a small park near Newcomen Street.

Footsteps again. This time heavy and close behind her.

She turned. A man, bearded and scrawny, in a long, strangely clean white robe.

'It is for the wise to listen,' he proclaimed in a deep voice, brandishing a phone. He approached her, his movements jerky and uneven. 'The end times,' he said. 'When the shepherds of the desert fight to build tall buildings. That's how you'll know these are the last days. And look—' He was closer now, moving from foot to foot and waving his phone towards her. She saw a photo, some kind of skyscraper against a luminous blue sky. 'Dubai,' he said. 'The Bedouins have left behind their herds. This is how it starts. But only the wise will listen, lady.' His voice was loud, his phone close up against her face. 'I will not stay silent, you hear me? I will spread the word and they will listen . . .'

He was still stepping, hopping, and now he began to drift away, his gaze beyond her, looking to spread the word.

She watched him go, clutching his phone and murmuring still.

* * *

'The Hadith Jibril,' Aysha said, standing by the stove in the hostel kitchen and stirring a large pot. 'I'm amazed you don't know it. It's the Angel Gabriel — isn't he one of yours? Anyway, he visits the Prophet, peace be upon him, and one of the things they discuss is how we'll know the last days are upon us. And in answer to Gabriel, the Prophet, peace be upon him, says, when the barefoot shepherds on the hills get a taste for settled luxury and fight over it — like, you know, the order of things goes upside down.' She chose a knife from a drawer and began to slice tomatoes. 'And your man there with his phone — you can't blame him for thinking that maybe time ain't on our side right now.'

The kitchen was a bright, wide room with yellow-painted units. The afternoon sun filtered through sash windows. In the middle of the room was a long pine table, at which lounged a boy entranced by his phone.

'This is Sister Agnes,' Aysha said.

He looked up. 'Another nun? Like Sister Dom?' He went back to his phone. He was young, with short black hair, loose-limbed under a baggy T-shirt.

'This is Oji. He appeared at Euston station a few days ago. Didn't you?'

He looked up, gave a nod, went back to his game.

'He's come from Manchester. And if he'd tell us what he'd run away from, instead of playing on that phone the whole time, we might be able to start putting a plan in place. Mightn't we, Oji?'

He had gentle dark eyes and his smile was taut. His phone gave off squawks and bursts of gunfire as he tapped at it.

'So, what happened last night?' Agnes asked.

Aysha put down the knife. 'There's a kid here, Kezia, sweet thing. She's fifteen. She's local and she's got history out there.'

'Her pimp,' Oji said. 'He came to get her. Armed and that.'

'You know PC Alex Ramsay,' Aysha said. 'Our lovely community copper? She got her away from this guy. Sprang her from some awful flat. Kez was in a terrible state when she arrived. We got her medical care, calmed her down a bit. But then this guy came calling.'

'Told her he loved her.' Oji put down his phone. 'Girls, int'it. Believe that shit. So she says she wants to go out there. And your nun goes, "You aren't going nowhere, missy." So now she's locked in her room, and that lad is out there and he's well angry.' He moved his phone across the table. 'Your Sister Dominique had to go out there, stand her ground so that Kez could come back inside. Tells this lad she's a nun,' Oji said. 'My view is, she should dress like one. Then he'd have shown respect. You too.' He gestured to Agnes. 'Jeans and hoodies and shit. How's anyone going to know what you are?' He pointed at Aysha. 'She looks more like a holy sister than you do.'

'It's a headscarf, Oji. Don't mean I've taken up holy orders.' Aysha tucked her hair under her scarf, washed up the knife and locked it away in its drawer. 'Which is just as well, 'cos the danger money just ain't worth it. And now Kezia is up in her room accusing us of keeping her prisoner. Here, Agnes, here's Dom's handover notes.'

* * *

Agnes knocked on the door, got no reply, pushed the door open a crack.

'What?' The voice was girlish and rough.

'I'm Sister Agnes.'

126

'So?'

Agnes still had the handover notes in her hand. 'I gather your boyfriend has been giving us a bit of trouble.'

'They can all fuck off.'

'Who?' Agnes inched the door open.

'Everyone, that's who. I can look after myself.'

'Right.' The bedroom was small and bare. A bed. An empty desk. A chair, on which was curled a large amount of clothing — pyjamas, it looked like — from which emerged a mop of blonde hair and two blinking blue eyes.

'Why have they sent you?' the girl said.

Agnes sat on the bed. The pyjamas were pink with yellow teddy bears on them. After a moment she said, 'What do you want to happen?'

'Me? I just need to go back to my life.'

'How old are you?'

'I'm about to be sixteen,' she said. 'I can make my own decisions.'

'And what will they be?'

Kezia studied Agnes for a moment. 'I need to go out to him.'

Agnes waved the file at her. 'According to this, he isn't very nice to you.'

The girl coloured, pinched her lips together.

'Seems to me you're better off here.'

'You don't know nothing about it. None of you do.'

Agnes faced her, in the fading daylight from the windows. 'I was like you. I married the first man to show any interest in me, because I didn't know what it was to be loved. I mistook his control and his violence for love, because I didn't know what love looked like.'

Kezia shrugged. 'Why you telling me this shit?'

Agnes went to the window, glanced outside, drew the curtains.

Kezia spoke again. 'It's nice of you to care, Sister, but I need to go out there. He's waiting for me. Dom took my phone away, but I know he's been calling.'

127

Agnes took a deep breath. 'Sister Dominique has been keeping a note of his messages. They're not very kind.'

Kezia unfurled herself and sat up straight. 'I need to go out to him. You don't understand the first fucking thing about any of this.'

'Kezia — what power has he got over you?'

'What?' Her voice was thin.

'I mean, the man assaults you. He lets his friends assault you. What are you scared of that's scarier than him?'

The girl shook her head.

'What's he said he'll do if you don't go back out there?'

The room was hushed. The birdsong seemed to quieten.

'There's nothing you can do,' Kezia said. 'There's nothing anyone can do.'

'Try me.'

Kezia hugged her knees, stared at the carpet.

'Blackmail? Photos? Videos?'

A roll of her eyes. 'I don't give a fuck about that.'

'So — why go back to him? Someone you care about? Someone else . . . ?'

A sister, Agnes remembered from the notes. Something about a breakdown of foster care . . .

'Your sister?' she said.

A darting, upright glance.

'She's younger than you?' Agnes guessed.

'Esti.' Her voice was faint.

'And what's he threatened, then?'

Agnes waited.

'She . . . she's all I've got in the world. I promised I'd look after her.' Kezia's voice was almost inaudible.

'Where is she?'

'On the estate. Over there. Where we live. She's nearly fourteen. He comes calling. He takes her out in his Bim. Buys her stuff. Perfume. Shoes. Margaritas. He's a good-looking guy. Her friends are well jealous.' Her eyes filled with tears. 'She don't listen to me.'

'Who does she live with?'

Kezia shook her head. 'We ain't got no one.'

'So — you do all this to keep him away from your sister?'

A small nod of the head. 'He says, if I stay here, he'll have her instead.' She stood up. 'So, you can see, Sister, I have to go out there now. He's waiting. And when he stops waiting, that's the end of Esti's life.'

'Unless we bring her here.'

Kezia stared at her. 'How? If you send the feds she'll run, like I did.'

'Until you were too damaged to run.' Agnes looked at the notes. 'Is it this address?'

A small nod, again.

'Trust me,' she said.

Kezia sat, small and tearful and suddenly childlike in her soft pink with its yellow teddy bears.

'There isn't another answer, is there?' Agnes said.

'No,' she said. 'There isn't.'

* * *

Agnes made phone calls, left messages, took some food up to Kezia, sat in the kitchen eating supper as Aysha served out vegan bean stew and baked potatoes. Eight young people sat around the table, eating, laughing, swearing, playing music, teasing the other co-workers, Eddie and Dan, asking Agnes who she was, asking when Dominique was coming back . . .

'I'm here.' The voice was loud and merry as Sister Dominique walked into the kitchen. She wore a long navy dress, with a silver cross on a chain round her neck, and her hair was twisted into a wide blue hairband. 'Agnes, am I glad to see you,' she said, taking out her earbuds and bending to hug her. 'The rumour is, you'll be back here soon and we can work together.'

'Is it? First I've heard of it.'

Dominique smiled her gentle smile. 'Of course you'll be the last to hear. Sister Christiane has her ways. I've made up a bed for you in the little back room.'

'We — we may need it. Come with me.'

Agnes led Dominique into the office, explained she was waiting for PC Alex to call them back, explained that if all went well Esti would be joining them.

'Ah, so that's his power over her. Trust you to find that out. No wonder Winifred misses you at the camps.'

'She does?'

'Of course she does. I gather you got on the wrong side of someone.'

'You know everything.'

Dominique tapped the side of her nose. 'Nun telepathy.'

They sat in the thickening evening warmth.

'How was the doctor?'

'Oh, you know.' Dominique sighed. 'Blood tests. Maybe anaemia. Nothing terribly wrong with me. "Stress?" they asked, with a funny look, like being a religious means we can't possibly be stressed.'

Agnes smiled. 'Sister Birgitta used to spend her days with the Benedictines growing potatoes, she said.'

'Oh God, can you imagine? It would drive me mad.'

'We were discussing the paths we've taken in our religious life.'

'A path? Obstacle course, more like. From Freetown to convent school, a law course in Paris, which I failed, a *grand amour* that was a terrible mistake. And eventually, here. Thank God.' Her hand went to the silver cross at her neck. 'But you and me, Sister, we're the lucky ones. We don't have to be anyone. Out there, everyone's an individual. Their unique self. Their wellness, their self-improvement, their apps. People are burdened with having to be a self. But you and me, with our language of faith, of the holy spirit working through us — it lifts that burden from our shoulders. We can be small people, just doing the work of the Lord.'

She sat in the near darkness, haloed by the light of the desk lamp. 'And when I get angry,' she said, 'when it all seems to make no sense, the badness in the world, or when someone's made me mad, then this —' she held up her earphones — 'Simbi Ajikawo.' She laughed. 'Little Simz. She shouts my rage, Sister. I'm telling you, we should all have her on our playlist—'

There was a loud alert from the doorbell camera, a ringing of the bell.

They jumped up, ran out to the hall.

Aysha was there with PC Alex Ramsay. Next to them stood a small, frightened girl.

Behind them, feet running down the stairs, a voice calling. 'Esti.'

'Kez.' The girl looked up, childlike and tearful. 'Oh, Kezi — I thought they was lying to me, the feds. Thought they was taking me away again . . .' She began to cry. Kezia, crying too, enfolded her in her arms. 'Babe, you're safe now. While I'm here, you're safe . . .'

Aysha led them both away into the warm kitchen.

PC Alex looked at Agnes and Dominique. 'You do know this can only be temporary,' she said. 'Breaking all the rules.'

'We're nuns,' Dominique said. 'We know all about breaking rules, trust us.'

Alex smiled, patted her arm. 'Sleep well, Sisters.'

* * *

The hostel quietened. Esti was settled on a camp bed with her sister.

Agnes sat by the window in her room, thinking about tomorrow, back in the convent library.

Doing as I'm told, she thought.

She wondered whether she'd be followed again.

Her phone rang.

'It's me, Athena.'

'Yes,' Agnes said.

'Are you okay?'

'I'm at the hostel.'

'Oh, thank goodness they've given you something fun at last.'

'Just tonight. Dominique had a routine medical thing and I had to spring a girl from her pimp.'

'Oh, so much less stressful than libraries. Though you sound a bit fed up.'

'I've been thinking I'm not a very good nun.'

'Oh heavens, is that all? The point is, you're a very good human being. Much better than I am. That ought to be enough. Those old nuns of yours don't half keep the bar high.'

'And I keep thinking I'm being followed. I thought it was Medodzi, the young woman from the camp, the one whose brother drowned.'

'Guilt. That's what it is. Terribly bad for all of us. I learned some years ago just not to bother with it, so much better for one's mental health.'

'But then today, I really was being followed, but when I turned round it was just someone prophesying the last days. He said the Bedouins were neglecting their herds.'

'Hmm. I can see that's a worry. Lunch, then. That's what we need. There's a word for it, kitten. Epicurean. That's the one, and I'm a master of it. A dab hand. A sunny day in London town, a fun half-hour lurking around beauty counters, maybe coming away with a treat — did I tell you I found a fab new eyeliner the other day? Next time you talk to your prophet about camels, tell him it's so much easier than he realises. The important thing, if these are the last days, is to look one's best. So, lunch, tomorrow. I'll message you. Sleep well in your mean-streets hovel. I know you will.'

Agnes smiled at her phone.

Tomorrow, I'll be back on the 388 bus, braving pimps and prophets, to be reabsorbed into the quiet of the convent. But this — my mean-streets hovel — it's this that feels like home.

Perhaps the gossip is true, that I might be sent back here.

In the meantime, I'll do as I'm told.

She was aware of a wave of resentment.

I must ask Sister Dominique to find me a Little Simz track that can shout this rage.

* * *

The next morning, in the library, Agnes put on white gloves, dusted the painting of Christ with the two sisters, hammered a hook into the wall and hung the painting in a central place between two bookshelves.

Patricia strode past, her feet loud in their purple Birkenstocks. 'What are you doing?'

'Keeping this.'

'Oh.' Patricia surveyed the painting in its new place.

'They're allowed a worthless painting, surely,' Donald said, from his corner by the computer.

'Well, I'm not sure about that . . . You'd better have a word with your insurers . . .' Patricia touched the frame with one careful fingertip.

'Too late, dear. Agnes has realised its value.' Donald laughed.

'What do they know about that?'

'Its spiritual value,' Donald said. 'As a meditation on the religious life. Hence its place on the wall.'

'Exactly,' Agnes said. 'You must come and do a guest lecture one of these days.'

'Don't encourage him, for goodness' sake.' Patricia huffed quietly and went back to her packing crate.

* * *

'You look as if you could do with a decent carbonara, kitten.' Athena led the way into the restaurant, which was dark-wood panelled, with framed black-and-white photographs on the walls and faded red bunting looped haphazardly along the ceiling. 'Nic told me to come here and he's never wrong. Not about pasta anyway.'

They sat at a table, perusing the lunch menu.

'Nice outfit,' Agnes said.

'This season's colour,' Athena said, pinching at her burgundy silk blouse. 'And with these lovely chocolate-coloured trousers. I was going to wear my lime-green cargo pants, but at the last minute I put this on instead — anyway, Emil looked up from his laptop, gave me a thumbs-up and said, "Better. Less brat, more demure." No idea what he means, but so sweet.'

Athena smiled at the waiter as they ordered carbonara for two and sparkling water. 'Got to be sensible — a whole afternoon at work after this and I can't risk falling asleep mid-sentence with a client. Much as I'd like to.'

'How's the magic?'

'So impressive. Although, it does rather get in the way at times. I mean, toasting the two of diamonds was fun, but now it's stuck that way and sometimes I just want an ordinary piece of toast. I said that to Nic this morning, but he just laughed. Silly man.' She fiddled with a button on her blouse. 'So, you survived South London. And how's everything else? Any further on with your mysterious dead lady in the cellar?'

Agnes sipped her water. 'Well,' she said, 'your theory that Tillman Senior killed her—'

Athena looked up. 'I knew I was right.'

'The son, Frank, found a letter from a doctor about hastening a death. Something about medication.'

Athena was wide-eyed. 'He drugged her? Oh God, I was so right, sweetie, about him being at the heart of it all.'

Agnes shook her head. 'We're not quite sure. It sounds as if she might have been ill and wanting to die. And Tillman Senior might have been wanting to help, or something.'

'What does your nice copper say?'

'I've left her a message again. Poor woman — she thinks we're all mad.'

'Hmm.'

'You're right. We are, of course—'

'I didn't mean—'

'No, you're right. One of my fellow sisters, Josephine — she seems to have stolen a priceless icon from our chaotic collection. Or at least Patricia the archivist-turned-art-dealer thinks she has. Mind you, Patricia's just as mad as any of us.'

'Yes, I can see that.'

'It seems to have been added to our listings later, like maybe it was already in the house before the other stuff

arrived. And Josephine knows loads about it and she knew
Tillman Senior — Colin. She studied Russian with him, she
told me, but when I asked her about Celia she said she knew
nothing at all. And now Patricia thinks she's got it and isn't
saying, and early yesterday morning Josephine was in chapel
going on about the Mother of God and not really making
sense . . .'

'Hmm. Patricia may have a point. Ah, good,' Athena
said as two bowls of pasta arrived. 'This will help.'

They grated parmesan, twirled forkfuls, ate in silence.

'And are you still being followed? Any more prophets or
anything?' Athena asked after a while.

'Not today, no.'

'Like I said. Guilt. You nuns are good at that. Much
too good, if you ask me.' Athena ate some more pasta. She
waved her fork at Agnes. 'You need a ritual,' she said. 'You
need to get someone holy in to sprinkle water or something,
burn some sage, get all that bad energy out of the building,
it's doing you all in.'

'Donald said we should pray to St. Anthony for the
return of missing things.'

'That too. If I didn't have Emil, I'd try it myself. And
how's that poor wife holding up, the one with the Audi?'

Agnes sighed. 'You talk of guilt. She was saying she
should have known how troubled her husband was. I mean,
you'd feel that, wouldn't you?'

'And that ghastly woman from Calais knew them? All
very odd. No wonder you're weighed down with it all. Vale
of tears, sweetie. Anyway, that's what you need. Holy water
— you must have loads lying around where you live. And the
missing icon — if your St. Anthony doesn't come up trumps,
we can get Emil to find it. It's one of his tricks. Mind you,
he'd have to produce it with a flourish.' She laid down her
fork. 'To be honest, sweetie — and I feel mean saying this
because he's so sweet — but all the flourishes are getting
rather tiresome. The other day, he did this trick with three
cups, upturned, hid my car keys underneath. I really needed

just to get on with my day, but I had to wait indulgently with all these cups being lifted, the theatrical wave of the hand to show nothing underneath, and then, wham, the keys were behind my ear. Nic said they were up his sleeve, but Emil was wearing a short-sleeved T-shirt, so God knows how he did it. Then Nic was teasing me about losing my sense of wonder, but it's not that. I mean, obviously it's magic, but I was late for Simon in the gallery and it was rather a lame excuse.'

* * *

Agnes walked back from the bus stop towards the convent.

At the cloth house she stopped and sat on the wall, breathing in the spring air.

There were no lights on, no signs of life at all.

Stephanie would be at her sister's now, in the village in Hertfordshire where they go back centuries. She looked through the iron railings at the drive, the red-brick walls tinted rose pink in the afternoon sun. She thought about Adam walking up that drive — his drive. She imagined him feeling the heft of the house around him, the solid confidence of its Victorian forebears, his sense that that was what he'd paid for — that solidity, that belonging. A home to raise his perfect family.

Agnes hesitated, then went up the steps and knocked.

There was no answer. No sign of a baby crying.

A remnant of blue police tape wafted in the breeze. She sat on the steps, as if waiting.

For what? she thought. *The house is empty.*

On the drive, scattered bits and pieces as if someone had left in a hurry. A washing-up brush. A baby's hat, old and soaked through from days of rain.

She thought of Paula, striding down the steps on the night that Adam died.

A wisp of gospel music . . . '*Who's that writin'? John the Revelator . . .*'

What is it that I'm supposed to know that I don't know?

136

She pulled out her phone, checked for a message from Sandra. Nothing so far.

It was time to get back.

Next to the hat, on the drive, was the blue bunny. In her mind she saw the tiny brown fingers, passing it from hand to hand. She picked it up. It was cold and wet. She stroked its small head, tucked it into her pocket.

She left the house, the steps, the drive, the railings, the gate swinging open. In the street she came face to face with Medodzi.

'You,' the young woman said. Her trainers were muddier, her clothes more ragged.

Agnes faced her. 'You've been following me,' she said. 'Why?'

'I think you know,' Medodzi said.

Agnes reached out her hand. 'All I know is that you need a hot meal.'

CHAPTER SEVENTEEN

On the convent steps, Agnes realised she was still gripping Medodzi's arm.

'I won't flee, don't worry.' Medodzi followed Agnes into the convent, rubbing her wrist.

The kitchen was deserted in the post-lunch lull.

'Right,' she said. 'Food.' She put on the kettle, raided shelves for bread, cheese. There was a bowl of leftover soup in the fridge.

'I'm so glad you're alive,' Agnes said.

Medodzi put down her bag, a battered blue canvas hold-all with a broken zip. She eyed the microwave as it warmed the soup.

'They said you stole a dinghy.' Agnes put a plate of bread and cheese in front of her.

After two huge mouthfuls, Medodzi said, 'Stole a dinghy,' and laughed. 'Fighting off them gangsters to take their shithole boat.' She laughed again, took another large bite of bread and cheese.

Agnes placed a bowl of soup in front of her.

'But — you got here?'

'I was promised. I was promised I'd get to London and I have. I said I'd do it for Ged. He ain't here. But I am.'

'But—'

'Brought ashore, we were. Border control? Is that what you English call it? And then I ran.'

'Medodzi, how did you get to London?'

She shook her head.

'I can help you stay here,' Agnes said.

Medodzi spooned soup into her mouth. She looked up at Agnes, her face aged with weariness. 'If it helps you to believe that, Sister, be my guest.' She ate some more soup. After a while she said, 'You ask me about how I got here? I tell you. I flowed. Like the river that was once pure and now is red like brick, I flowed towards the sea. All of us. You make the river sick with greed, the people get ill too. So they follow the water to find somewhere they can drink again. That's all we are doing. That's all my brother wanted. A safe place for him. And for me.'

She ate some more soup. 'My little sister died from the sickness in the river. My mother died from grief. "Go," she says to us. "Don't want to bury no more children." We buried our mother. And then we left.'

The soup bowl was nearly empty. Medodzi looked up. 'You give boys weapons instead of bread, what you going to get? Young men, out of their minds they are, them with their big guns feeling empty in their hearts, and they look at the women and the girls, and they want to feel like a man and so they take what they can find. Then there is only pain and shame, and that makes them crazed and angry, so they have to do it more.'

There was something in her voice, something cracked and hurting.

'Medodzi . . .' Agnes looked at her. She was trembling as she stared at the table.

'Medodzi, tell me.'

The girl closed her eyes tight shut, as if willing herself not to see. After a long moment, she opened them. She shook her head. 'No,' she murmured. 'Nothing.'

She took a last spoonful of soup.

Agnes tried again. 'What is it that you think I know?'

Medodzi lifted her head. She studied Agnes, then shook her head. 'I was wrong.'

She pushed the bowl away, got to her feet. 'I'm going now.'

'But — Medodzi, where will you go?'

Medodzi looked younger now, and tall. 'I've come this far. Ain't no one going to stop me now.'

'Stop you doing what?'

She shook her head. She bent to her bag, grabbed a hooded jacket out of it. 'This country, man, so cold. I ain't been warm since I got here.' She took off her shoes, leaning against the wall. She pulled on socks, put her shoes back on, standing on one leg, then the other. She stuffed things back into her bag and straightened up.

'You could stay here,' Agnes said.

'In your house of God?' Medodzi faced her.

'It's still a house,' Agnes said.

Medodzi shook her head. 'Sister, your God of love must have his mind on other things. Taking us for fools. My gods, they sit in anguish and they watch the fighting and the killing and the pillage of the earth. And they're angry. They're waiting.' Her eyes blazed. 'And so am I.'

She slung her half-open bag over her shoulder and went out to the hallway. At the door she thrust out her hand. 'Thanks for the food.'

She left without looking back, walking fast down the steps and out into the street.

Agnes cleared up the kitchen. On the floor, leavings from Medodzi's unpacking. A single filthy sock. A cracked and empty water bottle. The wrapper from a chocolate bar.

She went to the office, sat at the desk. She left a voicemail for Sandra. 'Please call me. I know we're a nuisance. Not just Frank's letter. Now there's the young woman — she's been here, she crossed the Channel and evaded the border guards somehow. I think she's in danger.'

She fished in her pocket, remembering the blue bunny. She sat him on the office desk, patted his head. Then she went to the library.

* * *

The library was empty. Agnes wandered between the desks, trailing her hand along the warm, solid wood. In Josephine's place, a catalogue lay open. Next to it, there was a book, bound in dark red leather. Agnes noticed the Cyrillic lettering on the spine. She picked up the book and opened it. A large, square bookmark fell out — the photograph of the missing icon.

She stared at the Russian writing, wondering what it said, wondering why Josephine had left this here, now. She sat at the desk. She picked up the photograph.

The handmaid, at the right-hand side of the picture. Her hands raised in shock, her spindle of red wool at her feet.

She thought about weavings and untanglings, the tear in the fabric of the universe. She thought about the cord that ties us to our mother, to life itself.

She hoped that Sandra would call her soon.

She took out her phone, opened the red book, took a photo of the bookmarked page.

She wondered, as she heard the distant doorbell, as she got up from her seat, why Josephine had left all this here to be found.

* * *

DS Sandra Campbell was standing on the doorstep.

'Sister, this better be good.'

'An answer to my prayers,' Agnes said, ushering her into the office, offering her a chair.

'You mean, they work?' Sandra sat down with a shake of her head. 'Uh-huh.'

'Firstly, Medodzi. She was here. She wouldn't stay. She needs looking after. She talked about sexual violence. She never mentioned it before. The route she took, Agadez, then to the coast . . .' Agnes shook her head. 'We had a kind of makeshift maternity centre for the women and babies. The midwives there would say dark things. Medodzi is traumatised. She's angry. Her brother drowned. She's been talking of broken promises. The woman who ran the charity, our CEO — I think she promised Medodzi something and that promise was broken, and Medodzi has followed her here.'

'So, this respectable CEO of a charity is involved in people-smuggling?'

'I'm telling you what I know, that's all.'

'Go on.'

'Here's what I know about Adam across the road. This same woman, Paula Gerrard, is an old friend of his. It seems odd that she sought him out just before he died. And no one told you. When you asked his wife about his recent movements, no one mentioned her. But I am thinking that this same woman, our CEO, their old friend, called on them both and asked them to keep quiet about something. And she wants me to keep quiet about something too but I don't know what it is.'

'Let me get this straight. This woman you know followed you here and went to that house to see old friends. And then this girl somehow miraculously evaded all our border guards and followed her to London too, because she's angry with her for breaking a promise to do with her dead brother?'

'That's what I'm saying. I know it sounds weird.'

'This Paula woman must be some chick.'

'She certainly is.'

'Okay. Mr. Crosland across the road. Financial problems. He wanted to borrow? They've been in business together? She refused him? Is that like her?'

'Yes,' Agnes said. 'That's very like her.'

'Where would we find her?'

'I have her number.'

'Okay. Punch it across. I have a lot of respect where your hunches are concerned, Sister. However crazy they appear — with all due respect.' She gave a small bow of her head. 'Now, how about the woman under your floorboards? What was this in your message about a doctor and a letter?'

Agnes sighed. 'We saw Frank again, the son. He'd found a letter. I've got it.' She fished in her bag.

Sandra read it, slowly. She handed it back. 'So, what, he helped her to die? Like, she was already ill?'

'I don't know.'

'The son—'

'He didn't know either.'

'I'll talk to Toxicology again.'

'But . . .' Agnes placed the letter on the desk. She looked out of the window at the grey afternoon. 'I keep thinking, she still needed to have been buried. In our cellar. Under the flagstones.'

Sandra shook her head. 'Uh-uh. The more we look at it, the more we find out, those stones had been broken for decades. It was just the clay and those cracked stones. She might have fallen among them. And, if this poisoning is true, she might have gone into the cellar to die. That flood the other week, that was a river, Sister, a great force of water. Enough to wash away the London clay and lift them stones. That's what our labs reckon so far. There's nothing to say she was buried deliberately.' Sandra tucked her phone away. 'It's like them bones, in the Bible, coming to life. In that valley, all them skeletons dancing with the breath of the Spirit upon them.' She smiled. 'See, that — that's the kind of scripture I could go with. The fun stuff.' She got to her feet.

'But — the rest?' Agnes followed her out into the hall.

'Heaven. Angels. When my nan died, I was thirteen, and I looked at her in her coffin, looking peaceful as anything, and I thought, don't go telling me fairy stories about where she's gone. I thought, all I know is, she was here. And now she's not. And that's enough for me. I wanted to say to them, "Don't take away my sadness by telling me lies."' She touched Agnes's arm. 'Keep in touch.'

'You always say that.'

'I always mean it, Sister.'

* * *

143

Julius poured tea into two cups. The daylight, defeated by the rain, had succumbed to dusk. 'So, the police will look again at poisoning?'

'Sandra said she would.'

He sat down at his desk. 'My worry is, poor Frank is burdened enough with all this. It would be awful to have the police chasing him about Celia's possible unlawful death.'

'Let's hope it's history rather than crime, then.'

'And now you have tales of missing young women too.'

'Medodzi said to me, "You know." What is it I'm supposed to know? And Paula thinks I know something and I've no idea what. Something about Gedeon's drowning? Something about Adam from the old cloth house?' She shook her head. 'I've no idea.'

'How is the thieving nun?'

'Oh, yes. There's this.' She got out her phone. 'It's Josephine's book. It's all in Russian and she seems to have left it out for someone to find it, deliberately. I took a photo of a bookmarked page. Look.'

Julius looked at the image. 'Cyrillic.'

'It's from a book just like Frank's. Red-leather binding, all that.'

Julius held Agnes's phone and tapped at the screen.

'What are you doing?'

'Translate,' he said. 'You can do it on phones. Ah, there it is. Dostoevsky. I did wonder. He was very keen on icons.' He studied the screen. 'Oh,' he said. 'Goodness.'

He handed her the phone. The page was now in uneven lines of English. Agnes read:

> *. . . and she saw that her icon (the same icon of the Mother of God) had been taken down and was on the table before her, and that her mistress seemed to have been praying before it. 'What's wrong Mistress?' 'Nothing, Lukerya, you may go.'*

144

'I know this story,' Julius said. 'The woman, she jumps out of a window and dies.'

They listened to the traffic, loud against the rainy streets.

'What does she know?' Agnes said at last. 'Josephine?'

Julius read the page again. He passed the phone to Agnes. 'So,' he said, 'this missing icon was already in your house before the rest of the collection arrived?'

'Maybe,' she said. 'Then it got listed with the others. But maybe Josephine knows about its provenance, from studying with Frank's father. Even if she didn't know Celia, which she claims to be true.' She put her phone in her bag. 'Whatever the story is, it's thrown Josephine into a crisis. Patricia says we're all temperamental, but I don't think we're any more crazy than civilians, are we?'

Julius laughed. 'Mind you, it turns out even the most ordinary human life contains the extraordinary. Seamus the nephew came to me yesterday about this eulogy and said that his uncle lied about his age. Took ten years off his life, apparently. They've got the death certificate with a completely different age and now the registrar is involved.'

'Athena says everyone has got the wrong star sign now. She blames the pandemic.'

'Ah,' Julius said. 'Nice to have a proper, rational explanation at last. More tea?'

CHAPTER EIGHTEEN

There was supper, vespers, a Lenten hush about the convent, an absence, still, of Sister Josephine.

At last, alone in her room, Agnes called Winifred.

'What news?' Winifred sounded tired.

'Medodzi. She found me. I gave her soup at the convent. She left, again.'

'What?'

'She's angry and she's on a mission. And like everyone else round here, she seems to think I know more than I do.'

'Paula?'

'It must be connected.'

'Her brother. All that awfulness.'

'And . . .' Agnes said. 'She began to talk. I mean, really talk. About her journey as far as France. About — about how badly young men behave . . .'

'Ah. I thought it must be there somewhere. These poor young people. Getting to England is a small part of the whole trauma.'

'At least she's begun to talk about it. Do you remember her silence at the camp? And then after her brother died, she hardly spoke at all. And now she's gone, again.'

'I bet you nearly chased her.'

'She can run quicker than me.'

'Our knees. Don't get me started.'

There was a silence. Then Winifred said, 'You know, I've just thought, if she's really trying to track down Paula, there is somewhere she might go. It's just occurred to me. There was one of the nursing sisters, came to do a stint with the women's health centre. You might remember her — Gillian. Gill Hurst. A nice woman — she's in London now. I'm not sure she knew Medodzi, but she certainly knew Paula. She and Paula got on really well, weirdly. Do you remember? Like, really good friends. Strange. She's working for the NHS again — only part-time as she has a disabled sister who needs care and she needed to be back in London. I can text you her number.'

'Okay, thanks.'

'It's a long shot I know, but better than nothing.'

'And how are things there?'

'Oh, you know. The same. Rain. Police raids. Bonfires. Music. More dodgy trading in illegal substances. Hope, sometimes. Sometimes not.' Agnes heard her smile. 'I wouldn't be anywhere else.'

* * *

The city settled into its restless night-time mood. Agnes looked at the texted number from Winifred. *Gillian Hurst*, it said.

Tomorrow morning, Agnes thought. *I'll call her.*

* * *

'O God, why have you utterly cast us off? Why is your wrath so great against the sheep of your pasture?'

The sisters' voices filled the calm, sunlit chapel as they gathered for Mass.

'They set fire to your holy place; they defiled the dwelling place of your name and razed it to the ground . . .'

Agnes thought about crazed, angry boys trying to feel like men.

'Let not the oppressed turn away ashamed. Let the poor and needy praise your name.'

Agnes watched the priest at the altar, preparing the bread and the wine. She thought about the promise of the love of God. She thought about the voicemail she'd left for Gillian Hurst.

* * *

After Mass there was coffee, chatting, a brief catch-up with Sister Dominique about how the hostel was going. 'Absolute chaos, as usual. Kezia and Esti are still with us, and we had two young people sleeping in the lounge last night against all the rules, but it's either that or send them back out on to the streets — oh Agnes, I absolutely love it there . . .'

So it was later that Agnes found a reply on her phone. 'Sister Agnes, I remember you. Very happy to meet. Can you come to the house? I'm rather tied to my sister.' The warm, maternal voice gave an address. 'Just off Green Lanes, Harringay station on the Overground is best if you can get there.'

* * *

It was a busy Sunday afternoon, with bakeries and queues and people walking dogs. The house was in a well-tended terrace.

The door was opened, and Gillian was there, suddenly, vividly. Curly hair edged with grey, tall and upright, and dressed, now, in a blue and orange embroidered jacket, with heavy silver earrings. 'Come in,' she said.

The hallway was painted vivid maroon, the staircase a clean white.

148

'I'd suggest we go out, but I can't really leave Jen. She's happy enough in the other room, with her headphones and her music and stuff.'

She led the way into a wide, light kitchen. There was a skylight, ferns in hanging baskets, the green of the garden beyond.

'Coffee?' There was business with kettle, mugs, stove-top coffee pot while she talked. 'I listened to your message again. Medodzi,' she said. 'I can't say I remember her specif-ically. But there were so many. Was she one of the mothers? I worked mostly with them?'

'No,' Agnes said. 'She didn't have a child.'

'And Paula being in London. I didn't know she was here, no. But from the sound of it, she was just passing through. There's milk, there, and sugar if you want it.'

The table was made of plain stripped pine, with a blue vase of yellow roses at one end.

Agnes stirred milk into her chunky ceramic mug.

'Mind you,' Gillian said. 'There's this job opportunity, isn't there? Paula asked me what I thought, some weeks ago. We had a chat on the phone.'

'Job opportunity?'

Gillian laughed. 'You know how ambitious Paula is.'

Agnes took a sip of coffee.

'And you think she's followed Paula, this girl?'

Agnes put down her mug. 'It's something about her brother's death. She was angry, traumatised. As if Paula was something to do with it. I think it was after you left. Her brother, Gedeon, he got a place on a boat with some of the other men and it got into difficulties. The others got back to shore, but he drowned.'

'Awful. I imagine Paula was upset.'

Agnes tried to imagine Paula upset.

'Paula was always kind to me. Like with setting up the mother-and-baby unit in the day centre. Paula knew I'd done midwifery. She was so supportive, fundraising for proper kit — do you remember that lovely nursery area for the toddlers, all bright colours, those tiny chairs. Paula tapped some funder for that, I remember. Funny when she's not maternal herself. Perhaps it's a way of making up for it, although I don't have children either and I've never felt the loss . . .' Gillian topped up Agnes's coffee mug. 'So,' she went on, 'this girl — she must have paid to come here? Maybe there are people she has to see. They often get caught up in paying off debts in London and then they get into more trouble.' She stirred a spoon around in her mug. 'It's insoluble. It's all money, isn't it? The whole damn world of it. Deforestation, mining. Drought. Fish dying. Insects dying. All from human greed.' She spoke with passion, in the brightness of her kitchen with the orange and the blue and the yellow of the roses.

'Medodzi said the river in her village ran brick-red.'

'Exactly,' Gillian said. 'Extraction. Always. The rivers run with blood and the mine owners get rich. Trade, that's what they've always called it. Gold. Sugar, cocoa, cotton. People. Slaves. My grandmother in Jamaica, she would say she carried it in her bones. She knew the old plantation songs. She said, "The chain gangs that made the white man rich, he couldn't drown their singing."' She sighed, dabbed at a spill of coffee on the table. 'And she came here, made a new life for herself. Married my grandfather. "I became an Englishwoman," she would say, laughing, as if it was a joke.' She smiled at the memory. 'But it doesn't end, does it? Now it's just a different kind of slavery. Lithium. Gold. The mines are so big now, their drilling is all anyone can hear. Silencing the birds. Silencing the singing. And those of us living comfortable lives — we just block our ears.'

Gillian fiddled with one earring. 'Do you know, I read recently that the old path of the East Africa railway, built by colonisers for their extraction of goods, is now the same route as the fibre-optic cable that makes the rich world richer.' She touched her phone that lay on the table. 'And yet, here we all are. Dependent on the bloody things. It's a type of serfdom.' Her brightness brimmed with rage. 'It's why I left, actually. I watched these people arrive in Calais, in the camps, and I thought, I can give them all sticking plasters. Or I can find a political anger about the cause of it all. Become an activist. Join a campaign.' She breathed out, shrugged. 'And then Jen needed me anyway as our care arrangements had rather fallen apart. So I came home.'

From the other room came laughter, loud tuneless singing.

'Jen,' Gillian said. 'She'll be watching something.'

Agnes looked at the sunlit room, the solid pine of the table, the pretty ceramics lining the shelves. 'Are you glad you came home?'

Gillian looked at her. 'This was my parents' house. My childhood home. I look around it, at all these things, and I think, Jen and I, we belong. Those old photos there, of our family, that one with the dog, that old black-and-white one — the old armchair in the corner that our grandfather had, the special tea set that no one ever uses. The lace tablecloths my grandmother brought from Jamaica. We're Londoners, you see. All of us immigrants at some point, but we find a home. You too, I imagine.'

Agnes nodded.

Gillian went on, 'And I think about the people at our centre in Calais, and I think, that's what they've lost. The meaning of their lives. Even if you rescue a few things from the rubble, the bombs, the earthquakes — it's gone. The meaning has gone. So, yes,' she said. 'I'm glad I came home. It's allowed me to belong again, in a way that I needed to. And as I said to Paula, I'm easily replaced. We had a great team there.'

'Was she supportive, then?'

A shadow crossed Gillian's lined, warm face. 'It was rather odd, actually. She got very cross. Unlike her, I thought. I mean, I was very fair, gave her a lot of notice. But we had a handover meeting, and she was very strange. Went on about loyalty, as if I'd let her down in some way. Really very cross. I was quite disturbed, actually. I'd thought of her as a friend.'

Agnes considered this. 'She was never kind to me,' she said, after a while.

151

'Really? Perhaps you never needed her to be. I think that's what she's like.'

'What do you mean?'

'When I first arrived, I was out of my depth. I hadn't done that kind of work, I found it very challenging. And she sort of adopted me. Made me a confidante in a way, talked about her previous job — she was dismissed, apparently, through no fault of her own. She was adamant everyone else was to blame. Anyway, she took me under her wing and I appreciated it.'

'Did you like her?'

'I think . . . I think she's not easy to like.'

Agnes hesitated. 'She was instrumental in me leaving. And I don't know why. Suddenly I had to be replaced by a different nun from our Order.'

Gillian sipped her coffee. 'Perhaps it's nuns,' she said. 'Perhaps because your belief system is different from hers. I can see she wouldn't like that.'

'And . . .' Agnes hesitated. 'Now she's asking me to sign an NDA as if I know something, and I've no idea what it is.'

'Now that—' Gillian jabbed a teaspoon towards Agnes — 'is very much in character. A stickler for the rules, Paula is. The right procedure. We were always filling in forms at the clinic. Mind you—' she placed the spoon carefully on the table — 'she often didn't follow the rules herself. It was a kind of joke, at the clinic. She'd appear with all kinds of things from nowhere. Baby milk. Medication. Syringes. Once she appeared with a huge crate of intubation kits, far more than we needed. "It was going spare," she said. It became a joke among us, when stuff arrived. Extra morphine. "It was going spare," we'd say.'

There was a loud burst of music from the next room.

'Taylor Swift,' Gillian said. 'She's unplugged her headphones. I'd better go. It'll only get louder and the neighbours complain.'

Gillian followed Agnes out into the hall. 'If I hear from Paula, I'll let you know. And maybe she'll know about this poor girl. Although I fear by now that girl will have disappeared into the shadowy world of migrants trying to survive in our city, in the hope it's safer than where they've been.'

* * *

'The floods have lifted up, O Lord
The floods have lifted up their voice;
The floods lift up their pounding waves . . .'

Agnes joined her voice to the verses of the psalm. She looked at Josephine's empty place. She thought about the red-leather book with its Russian script, and tale of suicide and icons. She thought about Josephine's sharp denial of ever knowing Celia Danziger.

'Mightier than the thunder of many waters
Mightier than the breakers of the sea,
The Lord on high is mightier . . .'

After vespers, Agnes returned to the library. She knew, somehow, before she saw her, that she'd be there. Shadowed in darkness, ghostly in her long dress and veiled hair, she was standing, pulling at something between her hands.

'Josephine . . .' Agnes whispered.

She whirled, and something fell from her grasp and landed on the wooden floor.

'No—' Josephine cried out, her hands clapped across her mouth. 'No—' She dropped to the floor, snatched at something, which Agnes saw now, as Josephine gathered it to her, was a spindle and distaff, with a thread of yarn stretched between them.

'Josephine—' Agnes took a step towards her — 'you need to go to bed.'

'No . . .' Josephine was shaking her head, but allowed Agnes to take her arm, to lead her along the corridor towards her room, still clutching the spindle and its tangle of red wool.

* * *

Alone in her room, Agnes called Frank.

'I've been thinking,' she said to his voicemail. 'About love. About what people do for love. About what happens when people do the wrong thing for love.'

She clicked the phone off, and sat in the dark and the silence.

There was a knock at her door.

Sister Christiane stood there. She was wearing a silk dressing gown in navy blue and large sheepskin slippers. She walked into the room and sat on Agnes's bed.

'Sister,' she said. 'What are we going to do?'

'About—?'

'Josephine, of course. I saw you, just now, leading her back to her room. She needs help. We're in a state of utter negligence where she's concerned. What are we to do?'

'Well . . .' Agnes wondered what to say. About stolen icons, and Tillman Senior, and things weighing heavily.

'I've tried,' Christiane said. 'I've told her I'm ready to talk whenever she wants, but she's avoiding me.'

'It's the icons,' Agnes said. 'Something has awakened something within her. Memories. Doubt.'

'Ah.' Christiane smoothed her short grey hair. 'I thought as much. The path not taken. Heaven knows we all struggle, Sister.' She sighed. 'Which reminds me — you and I need to have a chat about what you do next.'

'We do?'

'I have a feeling that our work in the hostel is once again calling to you.'

A chorus in her mind of the hostel's noise — the shouting, music, laughter, the occasional fight, the sleeping bags laid out in the lounge against all the rules, two sisters embracing on the stairs . . .

'It's not as if you could be a librarian for ever,' Christiane said. 'However, Sister Dominique is settled there and also managing life in the flat.'

The flat. *Your flat*, Athena always called it, as if it had been stolen from her.

'Well, Agnes, we will need a period of reflection and discernment about your future. In the meantime, more urgently, there are the needs of Sister Josephine. Whatever struggle she's having with her religious life, there's no doubt it's making her ill. This is my question, you see. Do we get the doctor?' She looked at Agnes. 'Ah. There we are. You don't know either. A tussle, isn't it? Do we medicate for depression? Or do we pray for illumination? It's not straightforward.'

'Our foremothers,' Agnes said. 'The medieval abbesses, with their libraries of medical know-how. They'd have done both.'

'True. But Hildegard of Bingen could count on divine visions too. Such things are rather sparse these days.' She stood up, pulled a slipper back on. 'Perhaps a helpful saint will appear to Sister Josephine and sort things out for her. But tomorrow, just in case, I shall talk to our GP.' She touched Agnes's hand with her own, and then she went. Agnes heard the soft tread of her slippers fade away along the corridor.

The ring of her phone broke the silence.

Frank.

'Sister,' he said. 'About love. I've been thinking me the same things,' he said. 'And then, those things, they led me to the films and the projector. I set it all up, but, Sister, I don't dare start the whole thing rolling on my own. Staring at those old cardboard boxes with his neurotic handwriting. I can't face it. So, what I was thinking, would you and your nice priest care to come and join me? Tomorrow, if your God will spare you? I'll send you the address.'

CHAPTER NINETEEN

'I hope this is wise.' Julius was looking out of the window of the bus. 'I mean, we're hardly even in London here. Look.' He gestured to the wide, leafy road, its detached houses set back behind generous gardens, the shiny cars parked in neatly paved drives.

'Hydrangeas,' he said. 'Who'd have thought?' He turned back to her. 'At least it's a nice sunny afternoon.'

She smiled and patted his arm. 'They don't let you out much, do they?' She was aware of the glances of fellow passengers looking on as Julius in his cassock and white dog collar gazed out of the window in wonder.

'Totteridge,' Julius said. 'Who'd have thought?'

* * *

Frank's house was like all the others in his street. Well-maintained, neatly painted, doors in tasteful pastel colours, garden shrubs coming into early bloom. Agnes checked the address on her phone. They rang the bell, which echoed loud and electronic in the house.

The door was opened. 'Ah. Good.' Frank seemed to take up more space, standing taller in his own hallway. 'Come in. Come in, come in.'

He led the way into a wide lounge. There were two sofas in soft grey with maroon cushions. The walls were almost entirely lined with bookshelves. Odd patches of cream-swirled wallpaper peeked out in between. More books were stacked in piles on the floor.

Frank waved them into the room. 'Sit down,' he said. 'Where you can. Sorting out, you see. Takes forever.'

Julius lowered himself onto a sofa. 'Are these your father's?'

Frank scanned the room, as if seeing it anew. 'Some, yes. Most of it's just mine. A long life, you see — stuff accrues, doesn't it?' He looked at Julius. 'Although, for you people, perhaps less so.'

'We try,' Julius said. 'Not to gather up treasures where the moth and rust can get them.'

Frank smiled. 'Don't get me started on moth,' he said. 'Tea? Coffee? Bourbon? Irish whiskey, Father?'

They shared a smile. 'Coffee, perhaps,' Julius said.

Frank disappeared into the kitchen.

The French windows were framed each side with ornate curtains in heavy maroon. Sunlight flickered through tall poplar trees beyond the long garden.

Bookshelves lined the room, solid with titles. Some old, leather-bound, muted lettering in Cyrillic and English. Some younger, livelier, splashed with colour. Julius perused the shelves. Agnes sat on one of the wide, faded sofas. In a corner of the room, Frank had set up a projector and a screen.

Frank carried a tray into the living room. His gaze followed Julius's.

'Chandler,' Julius said. 'And Hammett too?'

'I love them both.'

'Great writers.' Julius took a book from the shelf, flicked through the pages.

Frank watched him, smiling. 'So,' he said. 'Did you spend your time in the seminary reading *Celebrated Criminal Cases of America*?'

Julius laughed. 'Nothing else to read. That, and *Lives of the Great Saints*.'

'Ah, yes,' Frank said. 'Similarities there, of course.'

Julius picked another book from the shelves. '*The Long Goodbye* — it looks like an early edition?'

'Some of the hardbacks, yes. I'm a bit of a collector.'

'I'd be just the same given the chance,' Julius said. 'It's as well I've taken vows of poverty.'

He replaced the book and sat down next to Agnes. She looked from one man to the other and wondered how it was that Julius could always surprise her after all these years.

The coffee cups were small and bright with matching saucers. Agnes balanced hers carefully, took a sip.

'These films,' she said.

'Ah. Yes,' Frank said.

Julius was flicking through another book. 'There's an apposite quote here somewhere. About letters from dead men being silent. Can't find it though.'

Frank looked across at him and smiled. 'It's not in that one.'

'Perhaps we should watch these films,' Agnes said. 'If Julius has finished with his *lectio divina*.'

An amused glance between the two men. Frank stood up, went to the projector. 'I got as far as winding the darn thing in, and then I gave up. Silent, they are, no sound. But colour. Super 8.'

He drew the heavy curtains.

He flicked a loud switch.

There was a rhythmic clicking, a flash of leader tape, and then there it was — a silent flutter of images. Blue sea. White sand. Sky.

'The seaside,' Frank said. 'A holiday. Oh God, look, that's me.' There was a boy in shorts and hand-knitted jersey looking at the ground, holding a ball. 'He probably wanted me to play some awful game with it which I was bound to lose.'

The camera moved. A woman was sitting on a tartan rug. She looked up, smiled, waved.

'My mother.' Frank's voice was tight.

The camera panned round. Donkeys led by a large, sullen woman. Excited children, a man playing a banjo. Then the reel ran out.

Frank switched it off.

'I've never looked at them,' he said. 'Never wanted to. It's only now, when . . . they've become clues.'

'Sam Spade would have something to say about that,' Julius said.

A nod from Frank. 'Okay, here goes. This one.' He picked up a box, flinched, wound the film through the head. In the dim light, Agnes saw a name written on the box.

Here goes, she thought.

The first images were stills, close-ups of pages of text, handwritten in Cyrillic.

'I wonder why he needed a record,' Frank said. 'This is his work. The texts from which he made his translations.'

Then, brightness. Colour. Icons.

Angels, heaven, hell, saints.

'Why . . . ?' Frank murmured. 'Why record all this . . . ?'

The Annunciation. The Angel. The Mother of God. The handmaid with the dropped spindle of red wool.

'That's — that's ours.' Agnes's voice broke through the rhythmic clicking. 'That's the one that's missing.'

'Are you sure?'

The image hovered on the screen.

Agnes stared at it. 'It's not with the others. Patricia thinks Sister Josephine has stolen it.'

Frank paused the reel. 'That? There must be many like it, surely?'

The image juddered in the projector's beam.

'It looks just the same. We have a photo of it, like that. It's in the catalogues, but no one knows where it came from. The rest came from the Sussex house.'

Frank looked at the image. 'Celia's work,' he said. 'The study of icons. Neither of them religious, but both obsessed with all things Russian.'

The film played on.

More frontispieces. More Russian writing. A wobble, a gap. Then black.

A man, smiling, shy, wearing a soft black hat.

'That's my father,' Frank said. 'But — he never smiled.'

He leaned forward, stared at the screen. 'She must have grabbed the camera.'

The image wobbled. The man was laughing, reaching towards the camera.

'He was never like that.'

More wobbles, and then a new image.

A woman. A red dress. Blue scarf at her neck. A curtain of auburn hair, hiding a shy smile. Then she put her hand over the lens and there was black.

The reel ran out.

They sat in silence. Frank got up and drew the curtains, and a fidgety sunlight filled the room through the poplar trees.

Frank spoke. 'So strange to see him again. He never liked me, you see.' He turned to Julius. 'You'll no doubt find a Chandler quote about fathers and sons.'

Agnes picked up one of the boxes. 'Sister Josephine,' she said, brushing dust with a fingertip. 'She knew your father. She's not at all well. Whatever happened with Celia — and the icon — it seems to be connected to this.' She put the box down. 'There's a book she's carrying around. Russian. We've got a photo of it, me and Julius. Look. And Julius did a translate thing on my phone. It says this.' She read from her screen. '. . . *and she saw that her icon (the same icon of the Mother of God) had been taken down and was on the table before her, and that her mistress seemed to have been praying before it . . .*'

Frank sat completely still.

160

After a moment he said, '*Krotkaya*. Translated as *The Meek One*. A short story. A woman commits suicide holding an icon.' He took a long breath. 'The bones. In your cellar. Was there an icon with them?'

In her mind she saw the cellar. In her mind, the image of an icon, shining among the grit and the dust and the debris — and then what? Taken up by someone — who? — who adds it to a box of old books, which then came to be catalogued by an order of nuns who took over the house . . .

'It seems very unlikely,' she said.

'If your nun knew my dad . . .' Frank sat up, massaged his right shoulder with his left hand. 'He only loved Celia. Of that I'm sure. And,' he went on, 'if my father had ever owned an icon, it would be packed away carefully with all this.' He tilted his head towards the boxes of film. 'It wouldn't have ended up in your cellar.' He got up and began to pack away the projector. 'This whole business raises more questions than it answers.'

'When you said your father was guilty,' Agnes said. 'I mean, that letter from the doctor. If she wanted to die . . . ?'

'So, he helped her?' Frank faced her, standing in the middle of the room. 'I keep thinking how odd it is. How you can know something and not know it at the same time. I bet one of your wise old monks has said something about it in a book.' He began to fold the screen into its tripod. 'All I have, now, all I've ended up with — is a necropolis, a city of the dead.' He tapped the film boxes. 'Here they are, walking, laughing, sitting on rugs, watching donkey rides. And I'm with them too. My past, fixed in acetate. A little boy, losing at catch.' He laid the screen down on the floor. 'Perhaps we should leave the whole thing behind. Let them all rest in peace.'

Agnes and Julius were standing up, gathering coats. 'The thing is,' she said, 'Josephine is very troubled. There's something in all this that is causing her great pain. She says sometimes she can hardly breathe.'

161

Frank nodded. 'I know that feeling.'

'And,' Agnes went on, 'I'm supposed to get this icon back from her. If she's got it.'

Julius adjusted his collar. 'There's a quote, isn't there?' he said. 'Something about asking a dog to let go of a rabbit — how it's not the natural thing. I'm afraid that's like asking Agnes to give up on this case.'

Frank smiled, then laughed. 'Who'd have thought a priest would know his Chandler so well?'

Agnes took Julius's arm. 'Oh, do stop it, you two.'

* * *

They sat on the top deck of the bus as they headed back into the city. 'What a nice man,' Julius said, gazing out at the leafy streets, the branches that from time to time brushed against the grimy windows.

'After all these years,' Agnes said, 'you never fail to surprise me.'

'Keeps a marriage young, you see,' he said.

'Except we're not.'

'Not married? Or not young?'

She laughed. 'Certainly not married.'

'It would never have lasted,' he said. 'You'd have seen through me. And if I could think of an American noir saying in support of that, I would quote it now. Perhaps I should work one into my eulogy.'

'How's it going?'

Julius touched the window, traced a fingertip through the city's grime. 'I had another one,' he said. 'Day before yesterday. A man came to see me. Jimmy, he was called. He said he and Gerry used to clean windows together as a sideline. Anyway, he says to me, "Bet you ain't never played cards with him," and I had to admit I hadn't. So then he says, "Your Gerry there was either crooked or a genius. The stakes he'd play for. Wads of cash — lined his suit with them, he did. Got his poor nephew to pay for the funeral, did he? Well,

162

where's that money, eh? Someone will find it down the back of the settee, and then what?"'

'He said all that?'

'Yes. Also, this Jimmy swore blind that twenty-odd years ago Gerry was making a living writing the wishes in Chinese fortune cookies. Gerry befriended a bloke from Hong Kong, down west, he said — Dean Street, was it? — had a work-shop up in the attic.'

'Julius, you're making this up.'

Julius turned away from the window. 'Oh, Agnes, if only I was. The funeral's in a week's time — and how am I going to sort real life from fiction?'

CHAPTER TWENTY

Once again Agnes found herself walking from the bus stop to the convent. The sun was low in the late afternoon sky.

Across the road, the old cloth house was busy with noise. A large white van was parked outside on the drive, next to the Audi.

Agnes knocked on the door.

Stephanie answered — a blink of disapproval, followed by a smile of relief. 'Ah, it's you. I thought . . . Never mind. Come in.'

Agnes followed her into the hall.

'We're off in a day or two,' Stephanie was saying. 'I guess we won't see you again. This place will be on the market as soon as we've got the insurance claim through and can pay for the damage. But who would want it, honestly? Perhaps your Order could move in — you're probably holy enough to outwit the curse.' She gave a small, awkward laugh.

Agnes looked around, at the packing crates stacked, neat and clean, against the stained hall walls.

'I suppose the flood did me a huge favour in the end. Although, not Adam.' Her eyes darkened with tears. 'Ghosts,' she said. 'I'll be glad to go. I'll be at my sister's for now — she has a toddler, she can do childcare and I can go back to work full-time. She says I'll be happier that way and she's right. She always knew me better than Adam did. She reckons I need counselling too, like the police offered — I didn't know they did that, you'd think they'd have enough to do.' She patted at her eyes. 'Because I found him. How it all looked. Flashbacks. You know . . .' She darted a glance towards the staircase.

Agnes took a breath. 'Stephanie,' she said, 'what did Paula want? When she visited you?'

Stephanie felt behind her for a crate, sank on to it. 'I wish I knew.' She rubbed the back of her neck with a delicate hand. 'She talked to Adam for a long time. In there.' She gestured with her elbow towards the study.

'You didn't tell the police about her? One of the last people to see him alive; they'd have wanted to know.'

A hesitation, a glance at Agnes. 'I guess . . . I guess I was in shock.'

'Were you jealous of her?'

She considered this. 'No,' she said. 'Not ever, really. She isn't the kind of woman who could be a rival. Do you see what I mean?'

'Yes,' Agnes said, 'I do. Another thing — how did Adam have that pistol?'

'Oh God. That fucking pistol. The police kept asking me why my husband would buy a gun. Who would he know? I kept telling them it was absolutely out of character. I said to them, "That means he really meant to do it, doesn't it?" Some people stockpile pills — you'd think that's the kind of thing a person like Adam would think of. But to find a local dealer and buy an automatic, like the police were saying — he must have really been thinking about it for a while.'

'Debt?' Agnes said.

She gave a small nod. 'It mattered to him. Success. Measured in money. I'm sure you people have all sorts of biblical texts warning against it.' She began to cry, suddenly, sitting there on a crate in the dim, damp light of the hall.

Agnes sat on a nearby crate. 'You need to go from here.'

Stephanie nodded. She found a tissue, blew her nose. 'It was here,' she said. 'When I got to him. Just there, by the stairs . . .' Her voice trembled. 'So much mess. Blood . . . and . . . like, a hole. I thought maybe he was still breathing, tried to remember how you do that thing punching someone's chest like you see on those TV shows. But then I saw how his eyes were, like, empty. And I realised he'd gone. But gone where?'

She looked at Agnes as if she expected an answer.

'Well . . .' Agnes said, marshalling clumsy notions of a hereafter.

'Counselling. Like my sister says. Like the police suggested, once they'd stopped treating me as a suspect. Post-traumatic stress. They gave me a card with a phone number on it. Do you think anyone actually calls it?'

Her eyes darted, as she fidgeted on her crate. 'My sister,' she said. 'Her house. Untidy. Toys everywhere. And hamsters, ghastly things in little cages. But, do you know, Amy has the kind of dishwasher that opens itself when it's finished? And she says I can go back to work. It'll do me good, she says. She'll do the childcare. I can wear my usual clothes, workwear, you know, not this stuff . . .'

Agnes looked at this well-cut and expensive stuff, and wondered what workwear would look like.

'I can be myself,' Stephanie said. 'But then I remember. And I think, whatever myself is — it won't be what it was before.' She began to cry again.

Agnes looked at the ruined edges of the parquet floor. She looked up at the high ceiling with its spreading stains.

Her phone chirruped loudly.

A text from Paula. *I'll pick up those papers tomorrow. See you about two if that suits.*

Agnes put her phone down. 'Paula's coming to see me tomorrow.'

Stephanie lifted her head. 'Oh God, poor you. What does she want?'

'It's to do with me leaving the charity in Calais.'

'At least she's not bothering me anymore. I mean, she was always Adam's friend; we were never close. You know, she called me the other day — it was really weird. She went on about condolences and paying her respects. I don't know why; she knows I don't even like her. I thought maybe she feels guilty — like, if Adam did ask her for money and she refused, and then he goes and does what he did . . . I thought perhaps she felt responsible. And then I thought, she never feels responsible. The only person she cares about is herself.' She stood up. 'Oh God, I sound really mean. I just want to be the person I was before . . . before all this.' She gestured to the space around her, the damp, the crates, the damaged floor, the perfect life her husband had thought he'd buy, the ending of it all.

Agnes gave her a hug, and then left.

Out in the street, she texted Paula. *2 p.m. fine.*

CHAPTER TWENTY-ONE

Tuesday morning started with stale cereal and a text from Paula confirming their meeting.

'Oh God, sweetie,' Athena said, in the café on the corner an hour later. 'That's a terrible start to a day. Almost as bad as mine. I went to the cutlery drawer and there wasn't a single fork in there — all of them gone. And then Emil insisted on doing a thing with a large silk scarf waved over the drawer and they all reappeared. Impressive, of course, but I was trying to make scrambled eggs at the time. *So* annoying. And then Nic teased me yet again about losing my sense of wonder, which didn't help at all.' She picked up the menu.

'I sat opposite silent, non-eating Sister Josephine with a plate of old cornflakes.'

'Coffee, then. And lots of it. You'll need to keep your strength up for that awful woman.'

'She's after something and I don't know what. Gillian, the woman I met on Sunday — she spoke so highly of her. Like they were best friends. Strange.'

'She must be selective about who she counts as a friend.'

'Nuns, Gillian said. We challenge her, apparently.'

'Oh heavens, kitten, I know the feeling. Whipped cream, I think,' she said as the waitress took their order.

'All I know is this,' Agnes said. 'She knew Adam across the road. She visited him the evening he died. They were closeted together. Something about money, perhaps. Or him helping her get this posh new job in London. None of which his wife told the police at the time, but then she was in an awful state, not surprisingly. It was me who told the police once I knew. And then there's this business of these stupid forms. I'm supposed to sign them for her to pick up today. I could have posted them. Or emailed them, even.'

'You must have something she wants. But God knows what it is.'

The waitress returned with two large coffees, one covered with whipped cream.

'Will you challenge her?' Athena licked cream from her spoon.

'I'm going to have to. Julius said asking me to lay off is like asking a dog not to chase a rabbit.'

'Rude.'

'He was bonding with Frank, the man with the tapes. Both of them quoting old American detectives.'

'Oh, no, not crime fiction. I can't be doing with it. Everything gets solved. Not like real life.'

'We went to Frank's house yesterday. He showed us these two films. And there was his dad. Smiling. Frank said he never smiled. And Celia. The woman in our cellar. Standing there in a nice red coat, laughing.'

'How weird. To see the dead. Spooky.'

'And we're no further on.'

'See? Nothing solved. How's Julius's Irish funeral?'

'Well, it seems Gerry played cards for very high stakes and was very rich. And at one point he worked in a Soho garret writing the wishes for Chinese fortune cookies.'

Athena waved her spoon. 'Proves my point. Totally random. Just real life. Nothing neat. Nothing sewn up. Anyway, I'm sure dear Julius is equal to the task. And you're equal to the Paulas of this world.' Athena surveyed her. 'Although

— maybe — a bit of colour on your cheeks? A touch of lipstick? You are looking a bit . . .'

'Tired,' Agnes said.

'A nice satin mocha lip would suit you.'

'I was awake most of the night. After talking to poor
Stephanie. It's all a tangle, you see. And Sandra said the pistol that Adam used was the kind that's carried by warring
kids round here. Like, where did he get it? And Medodzi
is still missing. And Josephine, my fellow sister, is in crisis,
just when we're supposed to be packing up the collection.
Sister Christiane is trying to get her to see our GP. Josephine
is obsessed with the icons. She said she wanted to be an art
historian, but her ambitions were thwarted by poverty.'

'Well, in that case,' Athena said. 'She shouldn't be a
nun, should she? It's perfectly obvious. If your GP has any
sense, that's what they'll say.'

Agnes stared at her.

'I mean,' Athena went on, 'I didn't think people these
days became nuns just to have a roof over their head.' She
gestured to the waitress for the bill. 'Well, I'm right, aren't I?'

Agnes began to answer. 'It's about vocation,' she said.
'And faith. We have to be discerning about the path we
take . . .' But Athena was speaking again.

'It'll be that dead woman in your cellar. It's brought
things to light. Clearly, that old Russian spy bumped her
off. Tapes and films, and Tolstoy or whoever. And his son is
too under his father's thumb to admit it. We're both right,
you and me.'

Agnes reached for her coat. 'I hope we are,' she said. 'At
least Stephanie can get away from the house. She's packed
everything up, her sister is looking after the child and she can
go back to work full-time.'

'Someone's got to pay for those designer suits, I suppose.
Although, if it was me . . . I mean, your poor husband has
done what he'd always threatened to do — wouldn't you
hold your baby close?' She gave a shrug. 'Oh, listen to me,

what do I know — hardly a maternal bone in my body. Perhaps she needs to be with her City tribe.'

'Her sister has a toddler. And pets. Guinea pigs. Or was it rabbits?'

'Oh, don't get me started on rabbits. Emil appeared with a cage. Empty, thank God. But he was asking where you buy a rabbit in East London. Live, he said. Not to eat. He had a top hat in his other hand. I said afterwards to Nic, "Put a stop to it, please. You know how fast they breed, and that's without any spells." Oh God, look at you, glancing at your phone — you'd better go and find your inner warrior in time for that awful woman. Seems to me you have a lot to say to her. Lipstick or not.'

* * *

Paula swept into the office with a swirl of purple coat and an attempt at a smile.

'I do love it here,' she said, her gaze taking in the space, the cheap shelving, the printer in one corner, the ancient desk with the desktop computer squatting on top of it. 'So peaceful. It must be all you nuns. No wonder you were glad to get back here,' she added, flinging herself briskly into one of the two armchairs. 'So, shall we get started?'

Agnes sat down opposite her and took a breath. 'I've signed those papers.'

'Wonderful.' Paula held out her hand, as if to take them.

Agnes glanced at the desk, where the file lay ready. 'We have lots to talk about,' she said.

'Do we?' Her smile was thin, her face blank.

'I saw Medodzi.'

'Who?'

'You know who she is. I told you, she set sail in a dinghy. She's here, I've spoken to her.'

'Here — where?' The facade wobbled slightly.

'In London.'

'Whereabouts?'

'I don't know. I tried to speak to her and she ran away.'

Paula's face was once more a mask. 'I'm trying to remember which one she was.'

'Paula, you knew her. Her brother drowned. We had to prevent her from going the same way.'

'There were so many.' She sighed. 'We do what we can, don't we?'

Why are you lying? Agnes was about to say, but Paula's hand moved towards the documents that lay on the desk. Agnes shifted them out of reach and tried again. 'You knew Adam,' she said. 'Adam Crosland. He and his wife live across the way there. He died.'

The hesitation was momentary, barely perceptible. 'Adam?'

'You met at college. Stephanie told me all about it.'

Paula now wore a weird, lopsided attempt at a smile. She fiddled with the strap of her handbag in her lap.

'You know, of course,' Agnes said.

'Know what?'

'About the shooting. And you were with him the evening before he died. The police must have spoken to you.'

'No.' The word was emphatic. 'Why would they? I really don't know what you're talking about.'

Agnes thought of lipstick, a nice satin mocha. 'Paula,' she said. 'Why are you lying to me? I don't know why you've come here, but these documents are worthless — as you know. You encountered Medodzi. You knew her brother. And you knew Adam well — old friends, his wife says.'

Paula's gaze was taut and mean. 'I didn't come here to be accused — by you of all people.' Suddenly she was on her feet. 'I really need to get on. Shall I take that document?'

Her arm was outstretched as if ready for a swordfight.

Agnes handed over the papers in their transparent file.

Paula stood in the bleached sunlight, the file held between her hands. Then, suddenly, she sat down, as if the breath had left her, her expression frayed and weary. 'I did see Adam, it's true. We are old friends. I don't know why I said otherwise. Your news shocked me. I'm sorry. I did call there. Their lovely house. And this flood, it's done terrible damage, something about the way it was built. Adam was brought terribly low by it. I was quite worried.'

'Paula,' Agnes said, 'what really made you come to this part of London?'

Paula was still speaking, a faltering monotone as if to herself. 'I'll call there again,' she said. 'Before I go back to France. Check up on poor Stephanie. It must be awful losing your husband that way . . .' Her talking stopped. There was a silence. A twitch, a click back into place. She sat upright, turned to Agnes with an icy smile. 'Anyway, thank you so much for your time. I really have to go.' She stood up, holding the file.

'Paula — those documents you're holding — they mean nothing.'

Paula was heading for the door, talking fast. 'Non-disclosure,' she said. 'Client confidentiality. A formality, information systems, all charities do it . . .' She was brisk, nervy, her briefcase clutched under one arm as she brushed past the desk. The blue bunny that had been sitting by the landline fell to the floor.

Paula froze. She stared at the bunny. She bent down, picked it up. She held it in her hands, her eyes fixed on it. The light seemed to drain from the room.

She looked at Agnes, grey-faced.

'I refuse to be judged.' Her voice was faint. 'They spoke to me. The police. They had my number. A woman phoned me. A formality, she said. I told her what I could.' She looked again at the toy in her hands, as if seeing it for the first time. 'Perhaps . . . perhaps you gave them my number? It's the sort of thing you'd do.' She stroked the toy, an odd, maternal gesture. Then she handed it back to Agnes. 'I refuse to be judged,' she said, again, so quietly it was almost to herself.

Agnes placed it on the desk.

'Right. Well.' The colour returned to her face, to the room. A straightening of her shoulders, a smart tug on her coat lapels. 'Better get on. So sad about Adam, I'll miss him. And this girl, who you say managed to get here somehow. We must help her. Do you know how to find her? We must get her accommodation, I'll talk to the London office.'

The bright smile, the flick of the now neat fringe. She tucked the plastic file under her arm and went to the door.

In the hallway, she didn't offer Agnes her hand. A brief meeting of her gaze, then she turned and left, clicking on her smart heels down the convent steps.

Agnes went back into the office. She opened the window, craving air, breeze, light. She sat at her desk. She picked up the bunny, looked at the muddy marks on his soft blue head.

She thought about how you could know something and not know it at the same time.

She picked up her phone and clicked on Gillian's number. 'Can we meet?'

CHAPTER TWENTY-TWO

'I'm glad you rang,' Gillian said, later that day.

They sat in a café, a brief moment of respite away from her sister. 'A neighbour's there but I can't be long. Look, I've ordered this nice tea, real leaves in a pot. And there's cake.'

Outside, the blustery weather threatened April showers. People hurried, talking on phones.

Gillian traced a pattern in the wooden grain of the table. 'I was thinking about Paula and her can-do attitude. After we met, I thought about your question. Do I like her? And I thought, probably, if I met her now, I'd say no. Not that she's dislikeable. But — I don't know who she is. When I gave in my notice, like I said, she was really angry. Quite out of character. I mean, a true friend would be supportive of my decision, wouldn't they? And then I thought, maybe I was a bit naive about her. Perhaps I got taken in, with her always being so nice to me, offering me the odd cast-off from her lovely wardrobe, giving me dieting advice just because she was thinner than me . . . and all that very hard work for the mothers and babies . . .'

She topped up her mug from the chunky teapot. 'But there was a thing that happened — it came to me last night; I suddenly remembered it. It was before you arrived; Winifred was with us. And these men came to visit, high-ups from the charity, with the local mayor and his people. Checking on the day centre — as you know, we're there with their say-so; they could close it down whenever they like. And there were some trustee types too. And Paula was showing them round, being Paula, charming, quoting Martin Luther King or someone, talking about humanity, about cooperation. And she'd ordered in refreshments, and we workers were in the kitchen, and some of the delivery had been delayed, so we were late laying stuff out on trays. And then she appeared, alone — and absolutely yelled at this kitchen worker. A sweet volunteer, one of the English ones, hadn't been with us long. And Paula treated her as if she was no one. Like, she just saw a plan of hers going badly wrong and she wanted to be seen by these men as one of them. "Now I'm going to be shown up. Just fucking get on with it. Why are you so stupid . . ." Then she left the kitchen. The girl she'd shouted at put down her salad servers and walked out. I didn't blame her.'

She sipped her tea. 'Afterwards, when they'd all gone, I said to Paula that that was a bit unfair, they were doing their best. I was surprised, to be honest — she was so different in the women's centre, usually. And she said something awful, like, "What can you do with people like that? They need to be told." I said, "She's a volunteer, for God's sake, she's here because she cares." It was like she didn't hear me. I was quite shocked. I'm thinking I might have been a bit naive about her.' She ate a last mouthful of fruitcake. 'Managing upwards, they call it, I think. It's probably a good thing she's going back into business. Perhaps that kind of behaviour is normal in the City.' Gillian picked up cake crumbs with a fingertip. 'And there's another thing. The way she could source things. You know how difficult it was there, the authorities lurking, those police raids. But our pharmacy was always strangely well stocked. We joked about it at the time, but I'm thinking now, it was really rather odd. I was never sure where she got it from. Really high-quality stuff — opioids, pain relief. My co-worker, Gwen — she reckoned it was illegal, half of it. Gwen had worked with Paula before, in London, when she was on the board of a charity for ex-prisoners, and she said Paula used to boast about how it's great to know ex-cons as they can source anything you need. I thought it was an odd way of talking about her client group, and she was just as mean about some of ours.'

Agnes remembered the drowning. The trailer. The dead man. The weeping.

Gillian licked her fingertip. 'Brand management,' she said. 'Reputation enhancement.'

'Yes,' Agnes said.

'Well, whatever this new job is, it will probably suit her better. I mean, I always knew she was difficult to like. But — she was very good at her job.' She looked at her phone. 'I'm going to have to go in a minute.'

She picked up her coat, her scarf. 'Except there,' she said, getting to her feet. 'No one can be good at their job there, can they? It was beyond us all. The very existence of those camps is a failure. No one can turn it into a success.'

In the street, in the breezy sunlight, she gave Agnes a hug. 'Keep in touch. I hope you find that girl. It would be great to give her a safe place at last — God knows she needs one.' Gillian touched her sleeve. 'Perhaps we care too much. But there's no alternative, is there?'

* * *

After vespers, Agnes sat alone in the office, in the quiet of the convent evening.

She thought of Frank's necropolis, his city of the dead — the stuttering images, the splash of red of Celia's coat, the smile of Colin Tillman, strangely, briefly, alive once more. She thought about the page from the Russian story, the woman who dies clutching the icon.

But how does the story connect with anything? So, Celia died in our cellar. She knew Colin Tillman. But — does that make him a murderer? And is that what Josephine is carrying, so weighed down, so heavy-hearted? And yet, she says she never knew Celia.

She remembered Paula, clicking into place, walking stiffly out of the door. And Gillian's account of Paula — her fickle friendship, the strangely well-stocked pharmacy. 'Those ex-cons can source anything you need,' she'd said.

Even a Sig Sauer nine millimetre. The sort anyone could find on any street corner in Hackney if they knew who to ask.

The blue bunny was sitting on the desk. Agnes picked it up, held it in her hands.

Adam thought you could buy happiness, Stephanie had said.

What was Paula asking Adam to hide?

She saw, again, Paula's face as she stared at the bunny on the floor.

She saw, again, the spindle of red wool as it clattered to the library floor; Josephine's face in the darkness; the interruption in the universe, the breach in the order of things.

Paula returned to London, driven and desperate. And then what? Sourced a weapon from her former clients. Visited Adam on the night he died. And now — here she is, saying she'll call on Stephanie, tomorrow, before she leaves for France.

What does she have to say to Stephanie? What did she say to Adam? Whatever it is, Paula thinks I know.

A tough racket, Agnes thought. *Isn't that what Frank would say? Or Julius. Or Dostoevsky.*

Something happened at the camp that spooked her, that made her determined I should leave.

Medodzi has followed Paula all the way to London, all the way to these streets, fuelled by rage, by grief.

In her mind she saw the clay-dead hand dragging in the sand. Heard a woman's wail: 'My brother. A promise broken.'

Who had promised Medodzi her brother's safety? Who had broken that promise? Who would know the buying and selling brokered by the smugglers? And now this woman is walking the London streets, attempting to silence us all.

She stared at the blue bunny clutched between her fingers. 'You'd hold your baby close, wouldn't you?' Athena had said.

She put the bunny on the desk, picked up her phone. She called Stephanie, who answered.

'Agnes—'

'Stephanie,' she said. 'When are you leaving your house?'

'I'm back there tomorrow afternoon. For the last time. Loading the van.'

'Paula says she'll call on you.'

'Paula?' Her voice was shaky.

In the background, Agnes could hear a female voice chivvying a child, 'Come on, bedtime now . . .'

'Paula?' Stephanie said again. 'Why?'

'No idea,' Agnes said. 'Before she leaves for France, she said to me.'

'Oh God, what does she want now? She scares me, you know.'

'I could . . .' Agnes said. 'I could come across too?'

Stephanie's voice was washed with relief. 'Oh, would you? I don't like being on my own with her.' A small laugh. 'And you can do childcare — I've got to bring the baby as my sister's at work tomorrow. Don't expect refreshments — everything's packed.'

'Okay. I'll see you tomorrow.'

'Thank you,' Stephanie said.

Agnes looked at her phone. *I wanted to say, be careful. But what are we scared of? Someone who's capable of finding a nine-millimetre automatic pistol on an East London street?*

She settled the bunny in a corner by the printer.

In her mind she saw the broken canvas bag, Medodzi pulling on socks. 'So cold, this country . . .'

Stephanie hadn't told the police that Paula had seen Adam. *But I did.*

'It's the sort of thing you'd do,' Paula had said.

'I refuse to be judged,' she'd said.

Agnes thought of Sandra's workload, the ever-increasing pile of her in-tray. She called her.

'Sister,' Sandra said. 'What can I do for you?'

CHAPTER TWENTY-THREE

At two the next day, Agnes crossed the street to the cloth house. The weather, grey and humid, augured thunder.

Outside the cloth house sat a hired limousine, a driver at the ready.

Whatever Paula is doing, she's planned a quick getaway.

She pushed at the front door, which opened.

The hall was full of crates.

She could hear voices from the living room.

She walked softly along the corridor, opened the door.

The room was almost empty. There were two sofas, covered in dust sheets. Paula sat on one, Stephanie on the other.

Paula turned a flinty gaze on Agnes.

Stephanie looked panic-stricken.

'Ah,' Paula said. 'Agnes. Stephanie said you might join us.'

The air in the room was thick and heavy, difficult to breathe. There was a single crate by the fireplace; on the mantelpiece, a candle, a chipped vase. The French windows rattled with the wind.

Agnes wondered about weaponry.

Stephanie gave a nervous laugh. 'I meant what I said about refreshments.'

'I meant what I said about childcare,' Agnes said.

'Ah. She's asleep at the moment, upstairs. My sister's going to pick us up soon. The removals people are coming for all this tomorrow.' Stephanie gestured at the two sofas.

Paula hadn't moved, sitting stiff and upright on the sofa, still in her purple coat.

Agnes pulled the blue bunny out of her raincoat pocket. She offered it to Stephanie. 'I think this is yours,' she said.

'Oh, we must have dropped it,' Stephanie said. 'Poor thing.' She stroked its head.

Paula stared at the toy. There was a nervous tapping of her feet in their soft leather ankle boots. The space around her tightened.

Agnes faced her. 'You lied,' she said. 'You lied to everyone. You lied to Adam. And you lied to Medodzi. You made promises you couldn't possibly keep. And you didn't care. As long as your reputation, your brand management, stayed intact.'

Paula's voice was suddenly loud and angry. 'I don't know what you mean.'

Stephanie looked from one to the other.

'You know very well what I mean,' Agnes said. 'Your whole life has been about getting away with it. Well, I'm here to make sure you don't.'

Paula smiled. 'Oh, Agnes. You and your sense of drama. Nowhere for it to go, stuck with all those nuns.'

'At least those nuns, as you call them, know about human goodness — something that seems to have bypassed you altogether.' Agnes tried not to shout.

Paula's face had acquired a sneer. 'Now you just sound ridiculous, Agnes.'

Agnes looked at Paula's icy smile. She felt her right hand clench into a fist, as if to punch through the air between them, to topple her, like a spindle falling in slow motion.

There was a loud, explosive smash of glass. The French windows shattered as a brick crashed through them.

Standing there was a small, still figure, her hoodie too thin for the rain that had begun to fall, soaking the carpet's edge through the broken glass.

All three women stared.

'You,' Paula said.

Medodzi reached inside the broken pane and wrenched the door wide open.

'Me,' she said. She stepped inside the room.

Stephanie looked drained and faint. She leaned against the dusty sofa cushions.

'What do you want?' Paula said.

Medodzi faced her. 'You know what I want. You promised. You promised on my brother's life. And you broke your promise. I paid a high price. A price too high to pay.' She was shouting now, shaking her fist at Paula, still shouting as Agnes left the room. Agnes could hear her words. 'Drowning . . . Betrayal . . . My life left me when I saw my brother dead . . .' The words fading as Agnes reached the stairs, hearing fragments as she ascended, one step at a time, as she gathered the warm, sleeping bundle with the curly black hair, as she returned towards the lounge. 'You were the handmaid of the devil!' Medodzi was shouting to Paula. 'You made me sell my soul, promising redemption, and all I got was death.'

Paula sprang to her feet. 'Stephanie!' she said loudly. 'Police. We should call the police. This woman is prepared to kill.'

Medodzi looked down at Stephanie, who was staring up at her, blank-eyed. 'Not me.' Medodzi's voice was level. 'Not to kill. That woman is lying again. I crossed the sea for one thing only.'

Agnes stepped into the middle of the room. 'She crossed the sea for this.'

Medodzi whirled. She saw Agnes. She saw the soft, warm, blanketed bundle.

Agnes spoke again. 'This — this is what you want.' She went to Stephanie, bent to her and took the blue bunny, tucking it into the baby's sleeping bag.

Medodzi reached out her arms. The rage, the fire, faded around her. Agnes placed the child in her arms.

Medodzi looked down at the baby and began to cry. 'Mawuena,' she said, burying her face, holding the child tight. 'My baby, my child . . .'

Stephanie sank further back onto the sofa, her eyes fixed on the scene.

'I was wrong,' Medodzi was saying to the sleeping, stirring child. 'I did a wrong thing. But now you're back with me.'

'You agreed to part with her,' Agnes said. 'To pay for your brother's passage to Dover.'

Medodzi looked at Agnes and gave a tiny, tearful nod. 'I did a terrible thing,' she said. 'That woman explained it all. It all made sense. "A new life for your brother and then he can send for you," she said. Devil's words, she said to me. "What kind of life will your daughter have here? But there, you can start again. A husband, a home, a family. And your brother can have hope again," she says to me. I couldn't see another way. It was the only way — the only way to live instead of to die. For us all.'

She looked at the child sleeping in her arms. 'In those days, my thinking was awry. I would look at my baby and I would feel shame, because of how she'd come into this world. And what that woman there said seemed to make sense to me. Only when I had given her up did I understand what I had lost.'

Agnes remembered the silent, weeping young woman sitting in corners, refusing to eat.

'And then — and then my brother drowned. And I came to my senses. And I saw that a mother's love is greater than any boy-soldier's shrivelled hatred. And so I came to get my baby. And I followed that woman because I knew she'd lead me to where my baby is. I crossed the sea to get my daughter back. And now I'm here.' She turned to Stephanie. 'Your husband. Perhaps he died from the heaviness of sorrow at what he'd done. I know how that can steal the life from a man. I have seen it back home. And that woman there is the same. Chasing gold and finding only death.' She clutched her baby to her. 'I am going now, with my daughter. And none of you will follow me.'

She turned, hesitated. She went to Agnes and touched her hand with her own. 'Thank you,' she said. 'Thank you for your knowing. When I found you, I knew I would find my baby. Thank you for bringing my baby back to me.'

She walked out of the room, along the hall. They heard the front door open. They heard her footsteps fade away into the traffic's hum.

CHAPTER TWENTY-FOUR

Agnes and Paula stood in silence, listening to the rain as it washed against the broken glass. Stephanie was still seated, drained of speech.

Then Paula shifted, gathered her coat around her, picked up her bag. 'Ladies,' she said, 'I'm so sorry, but I've got a train to catch.' A flick of her cashmere scarf — a magic flourish, Agnes thought briefly, like a waft of silk to return things to their rightful place.

'Goodbye, Stephanie,' Paula was saying. 'Good luck, Agnes.' And then she'd gone, the front door slam echoing in the empty rain-soaked room.

Stephanie stared vacantly after her.

Shock, Agnes thought.

Stephanie turned to Agnes. 'Go,' she said, weak-voiced. 'Just go. Now.'

Yes. I must go. I must catch up with Medodzi; she has a baby, she needs help, somewhere to go, out of this rain . . .

In Agnes's mind she saw the spindle dropped in shock, the scarlet spill of wool.

No one had argued. No one had said to Medodzi, 'It's not your baby.'

Stephanie was on her feet now, standing in the middle of the room. Outside, a droop of jasmine branches tapped against the broken pane.

'My sister's due soon . . .' She gestured weakly to the packing crate. 'I'm going to Hertfordshire this evening.'

Agnes watched her as she ambled to the mantelpiece, picked up the scented candle, dropped it awkwardly into the crate. She looked up at Agnes with an absent smile.

'Your baby,' Agnes said.

Stephanie stood stock-still, then suddenly slumped, defeated, onto the sofa. 'My baby,' she said. She curled forward, her head on her elbows.

'You let her go,' Agnes said.

Stephanie looked clenched and weary. 'That young woman told the truth.'

'The adoption,' Agnes said.

'It was what she said.'

'It was . . . It was Paula?'

A very small nod. 'Yes. It was Paula. She thought she could solve everyone's problems.'

'And Adam,' Agnes said. 'Adam thought you could buy happiness.' She looked at Stephanie, hunched against the dustsheet. 'Paula — Paula bought and sold that baby.'

Then Stephanie jumped up, pacing, loud and angry. 'I was shouting at him. Money? You bought her? You bought this baby? I was furious, beside myself. Earlier that evening, when Paula came to warn us, she said that maybe people knew. She was telling Adam to have his wits about him, that's what she said. And that's when I realised. That it was about money.'

'Paula came to warn you. That evening that he died.'

'She called us. She said the baby's mother is running loose in London — those were her very words — and she may be armed.'

Agnes felt the shock of the words. 'Ah. So, that's why—'

'Paula brought the gun. She knows people, God knows who. She arrived with it, handed it over to Adam. "Just in case," she said. I was terrified. We were in the nursery. Adam put it down on the chest with all the baby things — it looked so wrong. A real, live pistol . . .'

Gillian's words. Paula being able to source anything. Knowing people from her prison days.

Agnes took a breath. 'How did the baby come to you?'

Stephanie shrugged. 'One day we didn't have a child. And the next we did. Adoption, Adam said. He said he'd arrange it all and he did.'

'No papers? Nothing?'

Stephanie was standing in the middle of the room. Calm now, oddly smiling. She spoke again. 'That baby was four months old, not even weaned. And he handed it over to me and said, "At last we're a family." That's what he said to me.' She gave a laugh. She reached out an arm, steadied herself against the sofa. 'I should have put a stop to it then. But I didn't know how.'

There was the pulse of early evening traffic. Agnes heard in her mind the whisper of vespers: *My soul doth magnify the Lord, my spirit rejoices in God my saviour . . .*

'Adam always wanted a family,' Stephanie said. 'I used to say to him, "Aren't I enough? We're a team, you and me." You have to be a certain person to succeed in our world and we both had what it takes. Working through the night, living on caffeine and stuff. Currency markets, futures — we'd bet against each other for fun. The power couple, our work-mates called us.' She gave a thin smile. 'But then something changed. He started going on about completing our family. I didn't know what he meant. "We are complete," I would say to him. It became an obsession. And then, all the trying to conceive . . . it destroyed something. We were angry. Silent and angry.'

'And so Adam . . .'

'Adam always got what he wanted. He and Paula were plotting her next career move. And he mentioned our problems to her. And she was determined to solve them. She was like that. And so there came the day when he laid that baby in my arms.'

'Stephanie — it was a crazy idea.'

She faced her. 'Too damn right it was. I said, "Adam you're out of your mind. We must find this baby's mother, we must return it." I was trying to contact Paula in France, but Adam wouldn't let me have her number. I even phoned your charity there, got one of you on the phone, asked if I could please speak to Paula Gerrard. Someone said she'd call me back, but she never did . . .'

A fragment of a memory. Sitting in the office, the ring of the landline, a brief conversation, a woman's voice. And then, Agnes's scribbled message on a scrap of paper. A name, a phone number — *Please call her.* She remembered now. How Paula had read it, slowly, then had smoothed it out and placed it under her heavy crystal paperweight with a strange, cold fury.

Stephanie was still speaking. 'I begged Adam, talk to Paula, tell her to get the child back to France . . . I was so angry in those weeks. I was saying, "What about my career? Do we hire a nanny?" He said he was raised by nannies and our child would have a loving family life. I realised then that he thought I'd give everything up. He said, "You'll get used to it."'

She sat down, suddenly, heavily. 'The rows we had. The nights with that poor child — me trying to give it a bottle, begging Adam to do something and he'd smile, and say, "This is our life now. We're a family." And then came that awful, awful evening, when Paula came here to warn us about the baby's mother following her. And she let slip that money had changed hands. She talked about the smugglers and what it had cost, and I realised that some poor woman had paid for her brother's passage with her baby. And with our money. Our money . . .' Her voice broke. 'I'd always thought we were at least rescuing an orphan, I'd consoled myself with that . . . I challenged Paula, and she went on about how all the rules were followed, how she's a problem-solver. And then she gave us the gun, like we were in some gangster movie. And then she went. After she'd gone, he tried to defend it. He said there were costs, adoption papers, that kind of thing. "It has to be done properly," he said.'

Typical of Paula, Agnes thought.

There was a scatter of raindrops against the twilit windows; a flicker of a thought just out of reach.

'Stephanie,' Agnes said, 'how much did Adam pay?'

'I was shouting, "Don't tell me!" I had my hands over my ears, I told him it was bad enough that he'd foisted the baby on me, it was bad enough that I had to go part-time with everyone at work cooing about my motherhood. "Steph, you're the last person I'd imagine to get all maternal, well done you . . ." People at work sending me little knitted things, like, who do they think I am? Have I changed personality?' Her voice was a sharp rasp. 'And now, I'm saying to him, "You tell me money changed hands between you and that woman, that we paid those criminals on the shores of France — for this . . ." We were upstairs, standing in the nursery, the baby was asleep through all the noise. I was shouting at him, "You bought her! You bought her . . ."' Her voice cracked.

'He was trying to shush me, went on about the neighbours hearing. I laughed then. "You're the one who spent millions on a detached house, no one is going to fucking hear us." I looked down at the chest, where he'd put that stupid gun. I think he saw, then, what I was going to do, and he began to run.' She took a rasping breath. 'He ran out of the room, down the stairs, me after him. I was shouting about him ruining my life, ruining our lives. "We used to be so happy!" I was shouting. And then . . .' She stopped, shocked, silenced by the seeing in her mind.

'And then . . .' Agnes said.

Stephanie's gaze was vacant. 'I . . . I keep reliving it. It's kind of here . . .' She waved a hand in front of her eyes. 'He stopped, he faced me. "Don't be stupid, Steph," he was saying. "You're not going to use that thing." His voice was all calm and kind of creepy like he did sometimes, like he had to be right and I was wrong, and I was standing really close up to him, still pointing it at him, at the side of his head — like this. And then he said, "You can't ruin everything. Our baby needs us." And so that's when I pulled the trigger.'

Outside the traffic stilled.

Stephanie took a breath. 'When he came home, all those weeks ago, put the baby in my arms, he told me all our troubles were over. What he didn't see was, they'd only just begun.'

Her eyes were blank. After a moment she said, 'We called her Isla. But — Mawuena. She always was.' She looked small, ash-grey, leaning crookedly against the dust sheet folds.

They sat there in the evening's silence. *Who'd have thought*, Sandra had said, *a crime scene in that lovely house, that parquet floor, blood and brains everywhere . . . You'd think he'd have gone out into that enormous garden . . .*

'I realised,' Stephanie was saying. 'I realised I had to make it look like suicide. Only my DNA and his, a really close-range single shot. I was thinking fast; you have to in my work. I checked the bullet wound, worked out the trajectory if he'd done it. Luckily he's left-handed, I'd have been in trouble otherwise — and anyway, I'm the one who found him. Grieving widow, my fingerprints all over the gun, I was in shock . . . Financial problems, I told them — all that was true, of course, only I didn't even know. Funny way to find out your husband was lying to you . . .' She gave an abrupt laugh, which wrenched into sobbing as she curled tighter in the chair, small and cold and broken.

Agnes went and sat next to her, and put her arm around her shoulders. After a while the crying ceased. Agnes passed her a tissue and she sniffed and dabbed at her eyes.

'And the worst thing is — all I can remember now is the man I used to love. Not the madness, the baby, the ghastly pretence, telling me what I think, telling me I'm wrong . . . All I can remember is how he was when we met. When I fell in love with him. On our wedding day. Dancing to 1980s retro disco under the marquee.' She grabbed Agnes's hands. 'Tell me — the woman I was then, and the woman who pulled the trigger . . . How can I be both those people?'

Agnes held the two cold hands in her own.

Stephanie spoke again. 'I suppose you'll have to call the police.'

CHAPTER TWENTY-FIVE

'And Medodzi just took her baby and left?' The convent office was dark and quiet, and Winifred's voice on the phone was loud.

'She walked out of the front door. I don't know where she is.'

Sister Birgitta appeared with a large mug of tea, a pat on her shoulder, a silent leaving of the room.

'And the wife? Arrested?'

Agnes took a sip of tea. 'Sandra, the nice copper — I'd already spoken to her. She came to meet me there. Stephanie just walked out to the police car, good as gold. It's almost as if she was relieved it was all over.'

In her mind Agnes heard it again — the loud, wet scrape as the front door was shoved open, as Sandra and two uniformed officers appeared in the hall, filling it with radio-crackling, boot-stamping noise.

A hurried exchange of words between Sandra and Agnes; Stephanie silent, head bowed, staring at the floor. Handcuffed, led out to a waiting car. At the car, she'd turned and looked back at Agnes — a long, lonely look. Then, acquiescent, she had allowed Sandra to help her into the back of the car and Agnes had watched her being driven away.

'And Paula fucking Gerrard? I can't believe that cow got away with it. Again.'

Agnes managed a smile. 'Sister, you never use that word.'

'She fucking sold a baby,' Winifred said. 'I knew she was wicked, but even so.'

'She thought she was solving everyone's problems. Medodzi pays for her brother's passage; Adam gets a child.'

'And she thought you knew?'

'It was that phone message that I happened to take. She didn't know how much I'd been told and obviously she couldn't ask. I'd spoken to Stephanie without even realising. So she decided she needed me out of the way.'

'And she's got away with it.' Winifred sighed. 'Like she always does. Well, at least Medodzi got her baby back. It's like the Annunciation all over again and you're the Angel bloody Gabriel. Typical of you, that is.'

* * *

'The thing is, Agnes . . .'

The library was clean and bright in the spring morning.

'It's nearly Easter,' Patricia continued. 'We'll be gone.' She picked up a framed icon. 'The seven seals. The symbol of Wisdom. And the sad fact is, your Sister Josephine knows more about all this than Donald and I combined, doesn't she, dear?'

Donald looked up from a heap of books spread across his desk. 'It's what I've been saying all along. Clever chap, she is. I mean, not for me to argue with her vocation, but if she wasn't a nun . . .'

Agnes heard Athena's words, again. *She shouldn't be a nun.* She heard, in her mind, her own mumbled answer about faith and vocation and the path we walk.

'Agnes, please talk to her.' Patricia was leaning against the library desk, her long legs draped in purple corduroy, an embroidered scarf looped at her neck. 'Her work is exemplary — her attention to detail, her knowledge. Donald and

I could really use her on our Liège archive project. And, with all due respect, she clearly doesn't fit in here — although I've said that of Agnes too, haven't I, Donald, with all your derring-do, out on the streets chasing ne'er-do-wells half the time, hardly like a typical nun, but you seem to manage your life here. Anyway, do have a word, won't you?'

Agnes agreed, that yes, she would. *If I ever see her again*, she was going to add, as there'd been no sign of Josephine at all for days. *For all I know, she's run back to Yorkshire and her sheep.*

* * *

Later that day, Sandra called in. 'We've arrested her.' She flung herself into an office chair.

'Paula?'

'Who else? We're not idiots, you know. She didn't catch the train, she hid out in some posh hotel in Vauxhall; we had a track on her phone. Thank God — trying to get her repatriated from France would have taken months. She's swearing innocence, says it was everyone else's fault. According to her she was just following orders, keeping the crime numbers down, went on about protecting the charity's reputation. She's charged with child kidnap and trafficking. And I'll be asking her about the provenance of that murder weapon too.'

'And Stephanie?'

Sandra picked up a coaster, a tatty image of the Madonna. She looked at Agnes. 'We'd have got there in the end, don't you worry, Sister. The ballistics report came through — the labs had been looking at the bullet trajectory, no way that matched with suicide.' She placed the coaster on the desk. 'Also, on the cold case, thanks for the tip-off about the doctor's note. To be honest, we've found no traces of poisoning so far. But the toxicology is ongoing.'

She took a sip of coffee, stared into the cup. 'Is this to do with you? It's actually drinkable.'

'I ground some beans earlier.'

195

Sandra smiled. 'You see, I was going to say, if you tire of the life here, you could always be a copper. But I reckon, with this—' she raised her mug — 'I don't suppose I can tempt you after all.'

* * *

'Oh, sweetie, I can't believe it. That poor girl. Can you imagine someone taking your baby? I mean, neither can I, but it must be awful. And that dreadful woman bang to rights too. Thank goodness.' Athena tore a piece from her brioche bun with her freshly magenta-painted nails. 'Oh, one weeps for them all. That poor young woman. But, come to think of it, the mother too. I mean, the non-mother, the posh one in her fancy work clothes. If I had a baby foisted on me, I'd feel murderous rage too. Poor cow. And banged up in the slammer too. No place for trouser pleats there, I suppose.' She glanced up. 'You look better, though. Got that ghastly woman out of the way. Justice has been done at least.'

Athena was in her burgundy shirt again, looking rested, her hair newly blow-dried.

'You look better too.'

'Oh, things are much calmer now. Just me and Nic. Emil's moved out. I mean, bless him, it was fun while it lasted, but, I have to say, it's a relief he's gone, sweet as he is. Now I just have to reorder my cutlery drawer. Buy a whole new set of forks.'

'He's given up the magic?'

'Oh, no, quite the opposite. The silly boy managed to find a real, live rabbit, did the whole shtick with the hat. It all went horribly wrong — the rabbit escaped, half the audience scrabbling around trying to catch it. But then some influencer who was there absolutely loved it, filmed it, put it up on their channel and now he can't move for bookings. A sad loss to microbiology, I fear. Drink up, kitten, I've got to get back to the gallery — I promised Simon I'd help pack the trawler-net sculpture for a buyer in Texas.' She ate a last piece of brioche. 'The odd thing is, the toaster has gone back to normal. I said to Nic, "How's that happened?" and he just smiled and said, "Magic." Silly man.'

* * *

The convent echoed with its own quiet busyness. Lunch preparation in the kitchen; from the office, a discussion concerning Easter Masses; from somewhere a soft sweet singing, a distant rehearsal of the anthems.

Agnes took the stairs two at a time and knocked on Josephine's door.

Eventually it opened. A tiny gap, through which Agnes passed.

The curtains were drawn. The bed hadn't been slept in, but was covered with books, drawings, framed photographs. Josephine's hair was tangled, her dress fastened crookedly. She paced to the window, her hands clutched, claw-like, in front of her.

She tugged one curtain slightly open. She faced Agnes. 'You can't help me. No one can.' She crumpled, sat on the edge of the bed. 'Sister Christiane came to talk to me. Went on about doctors. What could I say? So I said nothing.' Her fingers twitched in her lap. 'They'll send me away, I think.'

'No.' Agnes sat in the solitary chair. 'There's no need for that.'

'Tell me her name again?' Her eyes were dark and wild. 'The woman in the cellar.'

'Celia. Celia Danziger.'

'Ah.' A sharp in-breath.

'You didn't know her?' Agnes said.

'No . . . but—'

'You have her icon,' Agnes said.

Josephine stood up. She walked to the window. 'I fear they'll lock me away.' She looked at Agnes. 'Art, you see. The people who made those icons . . . their work and their faith, it was the same thing. But for me, here . . . that's why I can't go to chapel. I can't. I tried to tell Sister Christiane, but the words didn't come. When I'm in chapel, I want to cry out, "Who is this God?" I want to shout. You see, even saying it, they'll put me away, won't they?'

'No,' Agnes said. 'They care about you.'

Josephine shook her head. 'When I look at the icon, what I see is the paint. The lines. The choices. How to make Our Lady look like that, hold herself like that . . .' There was a brief blink of sunlight through the gap in the curtain. Josephine stood poised in the light, the fall of her skirts dove-grey, a tilt of her head, a look of equanimity. 'Like that,' she said.

'Josephine.' Agnes took a breath. 'I think you shouldn't be a nun.'

Josephine sat down on the edge of the bed. After a moment she said, 'How would you know? If it was wrong?'

'How do any of us know?' Agnes stacked a book on top of another. She spoke again. 'It's a matter of discernment. But — Patricia said she'd give you a job. They need your expertise. A collection in Belgium, apparently.'

Josephine stared at Agnes. 'A job — you mean, I could work . . . with the art?'

'You wouldn't have to go to chapel,' Agnes said.

'But my faith—'

'Perhaps the art is enough,' Agnes said.

Josephine looked at Agnes. Her eyes held an almost smile. 'Perhaps they're both the same thing.' Then her expression clouded again. 'But — I can't. I'm trapped. You don't understand. The woman in the cellar. I didn't know her. But I knew Professor Tillman, you see. I made a promise. I can't let him down.'

She cast a fearful glance towards her wooden desk, the three neat drawers, one with a small key.

Agnes spoke. 'Then, in that case — you have to meet Frank. His son.'

Josephine lifted her head. She gave a small nod of agreement.

Agnes closed the door softly behind her.

* * *

That evening she went down to the cellar again. The space where the bones had been lay swept and empty. And what of the missing icon? Had it been here too? Brought here by a woman in despair, a woman prepared to die?

In her mind she saw Josephine's desk, the locked drawer. *How do I explain to Patricia?* Agnes imagined Patricia storming into Josephine's room and wrenching open the drawers.

She stood in the dust and the darkness, and thought about stories and unravelling — the spindle's clatter, the chaos of red wool, the blood and the brains, and the curled parquet floor.

And Medodzi is still lost, still exiled, still illegal.

Her phone echoed through the emptiness.

'Hi, it's Gillian. I hope it's not too late.'

'No, it's fine.' Agnes stumbled up the cellar steps, into the corridor.

'I've got Medodzi. Here. At my home.'

'You've got . . . ? She's safe? How?'

'After we spoke, I thought I must help. I thought, there must be something I can do. I was thinking about Calais, the women's centre, and I realised we used to keep their mobile numbers, the clients', just in case — a confidential list to keep the women safe. So I rang them there, got her number. It was a long shot that she'd still have the same number, but it worked. She answered. She was outside King's Cross station, talking of sleeping rough in London until she could work out how you access services. "Don't be silly," I said. "I'll come and get you." I got my neighbour to sit with Jen, and I went on the train and got her. Her and the baby. They're both here, both fast asleep. I've made up a lovely room for them.'

Agnes heard the warmth and smile in her voice.

Gillian spoke again. 'I felt a fool. That's the truth. After we spoke, I realised how I'd been taken in by Paula. Like so many other people. That's when I thought I had to do something. I was angry with her, to be honest. I thought, she's not going to win this time.'

'They've arrested her.'

'Good.'

'Child trafficking. Kidnapping.'

'She'll say everyone else is to blame. Like she always does.'

'Not sure a judge will be so easily swayed,' Agnes said.

'Let's hope not,' Gillian said.

'Will Medodzi stay with you?'

'Yes. Absolutely. Obviously, it's a long path. She'll have to claim asylum; I know these things can take years. But Jen's delighted with Mawuena. I wasn't sure how it would go, but clearly we'll have to set boundaries about cuddle time. You will come and see us, won't you?'

CHAPTER TWENTY-SIX

Josephine stood in the middle of Frank's living room. Sunlight poured between the heavy curtains. She looked around her — at the bookshelves piled high, at the wide, comfortable sofas, the peace lily in its ceramic pot by the French windows, the low glass-topped table on which lay a small heap of books and some dusty folders. Then she looked at Frank.

'You are so—'

'Like him?'

She gave a nod. 'I hope you don't mind me saying so.'

He smiled. 'I don't mind. I can manage being like my father, as long as it's just on the outside.'

Her expression lifted, lightened.

Frank turned to Agnes and Julius, who were still in their coats. 'No need to stare, you two. I'll get the coffee on. Make yourselves at home.'

Agnes and Josephine sat on a sofa. Julius, still standing, browsed the bookshelves.

'He'll be looking for American noir,' Agnes said.

'On the contrary.' Julius drew out a leather-bound book. 'Pushkin,' he said. 'I think. In Russian.'

Josephine took the book from him and held it with reverent fingers. 'Yes,' she said. 'An early edition. Colin was quite a collector.'

She looked less thin, Agnes thought. Her hair was neatly tied and her long skirt, paired with an olive-green jacket, looked contemporary now, less like something from another age. At her feet was a large leather bag she had insisted on bringing with her on the bus.

Josephine flicked through the yellowing pages of the book, then placed it carefully on the table.

'Oh.' Her hand went to one of the books — a roughly bound tome of typescript, in English. She hesitated, then picked it up as Frank came into the room carrying a tray. She flicked him a small, nervous glance.

'That,' he said. 'The heart of the matter.' He put the tray down on a side table.

'His translation,' Josephine said.

Frank gave a nod. '*Krotkaya. The Meek One*, it became.'

'We've seen it,' Julius said. 'In Russian.'

Josephine looked at Agnes, the same flick of anxiety.

'In our library,' Agnes said.

'It was his,' Josephine said. She shifted on the sofa, smoothed her skirt against her knees.

Frank poured coffee, offered milk, sugar.

They sipped their coffee in silence.

'I didn't know Celia,' Josephine said, at last. 'I knew about her, but I didn't meet her.'

Frank bent to one of the folders and drew out a photograph.

She took it from him, looked at it. 'So,' she said. 'This is Celia Danziger.' She breathed, sighed, leaned back against the cushions. She cast another look at the photo. 'I may . . . I may have glimpsed her, once, perhaps.'

Frank smiled across at her. 'She was like that, Celia.'

Agnes took the photo, saw the carefree smile, the red hair blown across her face, the sky blue and clear behind her.

Josephine bent to her bag and drew out the Russian red-bound book from the library. 'You should have this,' she said to Frank.

She held the book out to him. 'It was in the house, I think. When it was the café, when people came and went. I knew it then, a bit. Because of your father.'

Frank took the book from her.

'I was studying medieval art. I became very interested in icons, and then someone told me about Professor Tillman and his Russian classes and how he knew lots of about icons, and so I joined them. I loved it all. I was so happy. And sometimes, we'd go to the corner house — it did vegetarian food, bean salads, terrible coffee.'

'No change there, then,' Agnes said, and Josephine threw her a smile.

'And Celia?' Frank said.

The smile faded. She held Celia's photo in her hand. 'People spoke of her. With admiration. With fondness. There were rumours, about the Prof. People expressed surprise. He was so . . .' She breathed out. 'I don't know how you'd describe him. So buttoned-up, I suppose. No one could imagine him having an affair.' She put the photo on the table. 'But it's true — he changed. He was different. He laughed more, he seemed younger. And everyone said she was an expert, that she knew languages, Russian and Ukrainian. And then some people said she was a spy and that Colin was getting himself into trouble.'

'Ha,' Frank interrupted. 'Those rumours never went away.'

'And then she disappeared.' Her voice was low. 'But by then I knew I was going to have to leave. My mind was elsewhere. Your father noticed it. He would talk to me, ask me what was wrong. I told him, about Mother, about having to go back to Yorkshire. He was very kind. He said I might be leaving the icons. But they won't leave me. And I didn't know till now, how right he was. But it took Celia's bones to teach me.' She stared at her hands in her lap.

Frank broke the silence. 'She's been haunting you.'

She glanced across at him.

'She's been haunting us all,' he said.

'I found . . .' she said. 'In the library. When they said they'd found a body . . . and that it was a woman . . . down there in the cellar. And then, tucked away in the library cupboards, I found a crate. Along with all the others. Books and stuff. But I knew . . . I knew it wasn't the Order's things. I knew it came from before. It had that book in it. And it had . . .' Her voice cracked.

'The icon,' Agnes said.

Josephine gave a small nod. 'And so then I realised the body must be her. And that these things were clues. But I didn't know what they were clues to. All I knew was that those bones, under our feet . . . I felt they were asking something of me. Weighing me down. As if I was entangled. My own past. My own story. All tangled up.' She drew her hand across her eyes.

Frank looked at Julius, who had been listening attentively.

'Don't look at me,' Julius said. 'If you want clues with no meaning, Chandler ain't your man.'

Josephine glanced between them.

Agnes patted her knee. 'Just men's talk,' she said. 'Take no notice.'

Josephine gave a small smile. She reached to the table and picked up the typescript.

'And this is your father's translation?' She began to read it. 'It's very good. You should get it published. Although . . .'

Frank met her eyes. 'Exactly,' he said. 'It's the last thing he actually wanted.'

'It would never be good enough for him,' she said. 'Always re-drafting.'

'Yes.'

'At least you've got the original now,' Josephine said. 'From Celia's things.'

'Keep it.' Frank smiled. 'Your library can have it.'

'It's not my library.' Her voice was sharp. 'I don't really belong there at all.'

Julius took off his glasses and polished them. There was a silence, an air of waiting.

Frank spoke again. 'I found this letter from the doctor. It's a copy, the police have the original.' He smoothed it out on the low teak table.

Josephine took it and read it. She handed it back to Frank.

'He didn't kill her,' Josephine said. 'I knew him. He didn't kill her.'

'How can you be so sure?' Frank's voice was loud.

'In those chats, when I told him I had to leave. He was preoccupied too. And he said he was worried about someone. He wouldn't tell me who. He said he feared for her. And he gave me . . . he gave me a copy of that story, as if it would explain it all. About the woman who dies, holding the icon. And he said, if ever I was to hear about a death, not to blame him.' She rubbed her forehead, looked up. 'I wasn't thinking straight, I was halfway to Wetherby. '"Promise me," he said. So I did. And then I didn't think about it again. Until the flood.' Her voice stuttered to a halt.

'But that doesn't mean anything,' Frank said.

'But — I have the last clue.' She bent to her bag, and drew out a square parcel wrapped in brown paper. 'Patricia in the library thinks I stole it, but it was never there to steal. It was hers. I know it was.'

She unwrapped the brown paper.

The icon was bright, vivid and familiar. The gold halo of the Angel, the matching glow of the Virgin Mary; behind her, the handmaid, her hands raised, the spindle of wool on the ground at her feet.

'I think your father gave it to Celia,' Josephine said. 'In the Dostoevsky story the young woman dies, clutching the icon to her chest. Your father gave it to her. He knew he was losing her. He knew she was ill. But what he didn't know was that she would leave the icon in the crate with the books and go into the cellar to die.'

'By suicide?' Frank said.

'I think maybe she just died. I think she was already very ill. And the cellar wasn't used then, the house was empty, and the London clay settled around her.'

Silence.

'My father's guilt,' Frank said. 'Heavy like chains. Like iron.'

'I think . . .' Josephine said. 'I think perhaps he was always like that. Celia could never have made him happy. The perfect love affair. The perfect Russian translation. Both eternally out of reach. That's how he wanted it.' She sighed. 'Perhaps she saw that too. Perhaps by intending to leave, she rescued him. Or perhaps she knew she was dying.'

They all looked at the icon, at the loosing of the spindle — the birth of God on Earth bringing about a rupture in the order of the universe.

'And my father never knew.'

'Your father.' Josephine looked up at Frank. 'Your father never would believe how much he was loved. By us, his students. By her. And, perhaps, by you.'

Frank met her eyes. He nodded, swallowed. 'Perhaps,' he said. 'Yes, perhaps.'

Agnes pointed at the icon. 'What do we do with this?'

'It must go with the others,' Frank said.

'Patricia will have me arrested,' Josephine said.

'Patricia wants to give you a job,' Agnes said. 'We just have to sneak this one back with the other two, as if it never left.'

'You need a magic flourish to make it reappear,' Julius said. 'Agnes knows all about it — her best friend is an expert.'

Frank looked at him. 'I thought you were her best friend.'

'It's a long story,' Julius said. 'And meanwhile, there's one more mystery.'

'And what is that?'

'The singing. On the tape. "John the Revelator".'

'Ah,' Frank said. 'Another clue, perhaps. But to what?'

'"The most divine knowledge is that which is known by not knowing."' Julius smiled at him.

'*Lives of the Great Saints*,' Frank said. 'Or Dashiell Hammett.'

Josephine looked at Agnes. 'Men's talk?'

'I'm afraid so,' Agnes said.

'Anyway.' Josephine began to wrap up the icon in its paper again. 'Whatever that music is, we can play it at Celia's funeral. I assume we're allowed to give her a funeral when the police have finished.'

They stood up to leave. At the door, Frank hugged Josephine. 'Thank you,' he said to her. 'Thank you for your care for my father. Even if the old bastard didn't deserve it.'

She smiled at him. 'I suppose that's what it is, to care. Whether anyone thinks they deserve it or not.'

'And as for you—' Frank placed his hands on Agnes's shoulders — 'I owe you a debt of gratitude. You're a darned fine man, Sister.'

CHAPTER TWENTY-SEVEN

For the next few days, the sun shone. The shops were piled high with chocolate eggs. The sisters practised the Easter anthems.

In the archive the three icons lay, one next to the other, locked away in the glass-fronted cabinet. From their silent vantage point they looked out at the crates, the final packing-up, the busyness of the archivists' last day.

Sister Christiane bustled past with a tetchy glance. '. . . the cost of insurance these days, it was bad enough when they added the risk of flood, as for having half the medieval treasures of St. Petersburg under our roof, that premium will ruin us, our cake sales won't touch the sides . . .'

Patricia glanced across at Donald, as the door closed behind her. 'At least we'll get something for this ghastly Victoriana, won't we, dear?' She tapped the boxes that waited by the door.

Donald polished his glasses. 'Apart from that Constable you've tucked under your jacket. At least Agnes saved the Velázquez.'

'Donald, I do wish you wouldn't. Not everyone shares your so-called sense of humour.'

'Well, poor Josephine here will just have to get used to it.' Donald smiled, rubbed his hands together. 'Today, we hit the road. Liège, here we come.'

Patricia turned to Josephine. 'Take no notice. We're going back home to Wiltshire first for a few days and you'll be our guest.'

'My wife might allow us to put the central heating on for once.'

Patricia tutted loudly. 'Do ignore him. The house is perfectly warm and you'll have your own bathroom. As for food, we eat very well. Mostly because I haven't been allowed anywhere near a saucepan since we married—'

'After that episode with the cheese fondue and the fire brigade,' he said.

'He loves to tell that story. You will no doubt hear it. Several times.' She placed the lid on a last box. She smoothed her patchwork jacket and surveyed the room, her hands on her hips. 'Well, it's been fun. Everything in its place. Everything listed. A job well done.'

'Any missing treasures,' Donald said, 'you can blame us.'

'Really, Donald, that's quite enough. As far as missing treasures are concerned . . .' She glanced towards the cabinet, the three icons gazing outwards in their line. 'It remains a mystery as to how that third icon reappeared. But then, it's quite clear that you nuns are rather skilled at mysteries. Unlike us ordinary mortals.'

'Perhaps,' Donald said. 'Perhaps it was thanks to St. Anthony after all.'

'I think . . .' Josephine said, quietly. 'I think it may also be thanks to Sister Agnes too.'

* * *

On the driveway, Josephine kissed Agnes on both cheeks. The spindle was tucked into her bag. 'I'm taking it with me,' she said.

'Wool and all?'

'The people of Liège know all about spinning,' Josephine said.

Agnes looked at her, at the brightness in her eyes, the colour in her cheeks.

'I'll be all right,' Josephine said. 'A new beginning. God knows where it will take me. And with these two . . .' She tilted her head towards the van. 'It could be anywhere. Donald says once we're on the A40, they put on funny old cassettes and we all sing along.'

'To what?'

'No idea. Italian opera? Hits from the sixties? Beyoncé? Let's just hope I know the words.'

Patricia stood by the van, directing Donald in loading a large cardboard box.

'I hope that's not our Constable,' Agnes said, and Josephine laughed.

'Here's your seeing-off party,' Agnes said as the nuns gathered on the steps in the sunshine. Sister Birgitta ran up to Josephine and hugged her. 'Oh, Sister, we'll miss you. But Agnes says you're doing the right thing and Sister Christiane says we have to trust Agnes's judgement.'

'That's not exactly what I said.' Sister Christiane rested a hand on Birgitta's shoulder. She glanced across at Agnes. 'It was more something to the effect that if Sister Agnes has a feeling about something, it might, just occasionally, be wise not to ignore it. Just occasionally.' Sister Christiane turned to Josephine. She kissed her on both cheeks. 'May God go with you.'

Josephine hesitated, held in her embrace. 'Thank you, Sister. Thank you for everything.' There hung between them something shared, a sense of discernment, the taking of a new path; a look of understanding and farewell.

Birgitta spoke quietly to Agnes. 'Does that happen to us all?'

'Does what happen?'

Birgitta looked across the drive to where Sister Josephine and Christiane were now standing by the van. 'Crisis,' she said. 'When you think you might have made a mistake. When those thoughts drive you mad.' Her words were strained.

Agnes looked at her. 'Birgitta — when did you decide to become a nun?'

'Me?' The freckled nose wrinkled. 'Well, back in Copenhagen, when I was at school, I read something about medieval abbeys. And then, obviously, we went to church, me and my family, and really it always made sense. And the more I thought about those old prioresses, the more it seemed to me that that was where I belonged. I began to research different orders, Benedictines, some of the Protestant ones. Went on retreat, a lot. And, you know, I hesitated for a while, I did a teaching Masters, came to London. But in the end, here I am. What about you?'

Agnes looked at her young, open face. *How to explain*, she thought. *How to explain my own journey, winding, branching, strewn with obstacles; a marriage in France, much too young; the terror of my husband's violence; the rescue, all those years ago, by Father Julius, who hid me away in an enclosed order until I could find myself again.*

'Me?' she said.

'Well,' Birgitta said, 'you always seem so sure of your path, your faith. I guess you always have been.'

Agnes smiled. She thought about the impending conversation with Sister Christiane about what she might do next, the waiting in quiet obedience that would be anything but quiet. 'Some of us have to battle with ourselves at times, to stay. And in Josephine's case, the victor in the battle is the woman you see over there.'

Birgitta's gaze travelled to where Josephine now stood, next to the van, talking to Donald, both laughing. 'A fight,' she said. 'I've never really seen it like that.'

Agnes touched her hand on Birgitta's sleeve. 'Exactly,' she said. 'Which is why you'll be okay.'

Birgitta looked up at her. 'So — maybe your equanimity was hard won after all?'

Agnes smiled. 'Maybe it's still a battle.'

Birgitta studied her, then gave a small nod. A distant bell chimed from inside the house. 'Ah,' she said. 'Summoned to the kitchen. If I don't go now, lunch will be late.'

'I won't be there. I promised Father Julius I'd help him with a funeral.'

'Dear Father Julius,' Birgitta said. She threw Agnes a smile, then went inside.

Agnes watched Donald and Patricia load the van, watched Josephine get into the back seat, Donald at the front, Patricia in the driving seat as the van made a sharp lurch towards the gate post, reversed noisily, screeched towards the drive. Agnes heard the beeping of several car horns as it went out onto the main road.

* * *

'No mouse mat?' Agnes looked at Julius's desk, at the snow globe, the pens.

'Gone. A fine lot of lollipops, my parishioners. Here one minute, gone the next.'

'Stolen?'

He shrugged. 'Perhaps their need was greater than mine. Now, how do I look?'

She looked at his purple robe, his white dog collar, his half-spectacles. 'You look like a priest about to do a funeral.'

'Ah. Good. Convincing, then.'

'What will you say?' Agnes said. 'Which version of the man will you tell?'

'To be honest, I've no idea.' He picked a sheaf of papers from his desk. 'Look.' He shook the pages at her. 'This is everything I've been told about the man. There's enough for five lifetimes, not one.'

Agnes felt the pages between her fingers. 'Julius, you've got to say something. What are you going to do?'

He smiled. 'Well,' he said. 'We'll all be gathered there, in the church, paying our respects, wishing him peace in the hereafter. And what I know is, there is one ending. One definitive ending. We'll all be standing there with the one certainty that Gerry Nolan is lying there, in his coffin, on his way to his final resting place. Whatever story I tell, at least we can all agree on how it ends. How it ends for us all.'

He took her arm and they walked out of the office into sunshine. Mourners were beginning to gather by the church door.

'Gerry lived his life,' Julius said to her. 'His many lives. Some true, some maybe less so. But he was loved. Chaotically. Haphazardly. As we all are. So, that's what I shall say. I won't mention the gambling and I won't get round to the estranged son and I probably won't have time for the property in Galway. Or the boiler. But — what I will talk about is this: I shall talk about love.'

* * *

Agnes watched him greet the mourners. There was the raising of hats, the shaking of gloved hands, the dabbing of eyes with newly pressed white handkerchiefs.

She walked down the drive, away from the church.

The woman and the child were in the churchyard.

There were flowers now, where there had been bare earth. Tulips. Violas.

The woman looked up and smiled.

Agnes thought about Medodzi, gathered into Gillian's warm home to raise her daughter in peace. She thought about Frank planning a funeral for Celia, with gospel singing and readings from Dostoevsky; and from Raymond Chandler too, if we're not careful. She thought about Josephine, her whole life stuffed into the luggage space of Patricia's van, singing along to Beyoncé on the A40.

Another ending. And a beginning too.

She thought about Julius and wondered whether he'd mention the Chinese fortune cookies.

213

She walked away from the church, through the sunlit graveyard. The old stones rested there, leaning, lichen grey.

She idled, reading names, inscriptions, poems, prayers. One was in Latin:

Sit tibi terra levis.

May the earth rest lightly upon you.

The woman was still kneeling at the small garden and now she called a greeting. Her child ran towards Agnes, holding something out to her in her small fist. A bouquet of spring flowers, pansies and pink primroses.

Agnes took the flowers. She thanked the little girl, smiled at the woman, then turned away, towards the drive, the railings, the traffic, the road.

She thought, *and we are still here.*

She found she was crying, without knowing why.

THE END

ACKNOWLEDGEMENTS

I would like to thank everyone who gave their time and expertise in the researching of this book: Dr. James H. K. Grieve, Richard Temple of the Richard Temple Gallery, Graham Bartlett, Sam Levitas and Lachlan Macrae. All mistakes and inaccuracies are entirely mine.

The religious texts come from *Celebrating Common Prayer*, Society of Saint Francis, Mowbray, 1992.

The Meek One (*Krotkaya*) by Fyodor Dostoevsky was first published in 1876. I have quoted from the translation by Ronald Meyer, published by Penguin Classics, 2015.

The fragmentary quotes in Chapter 19 and 26 are from *The Big Sleep* by Raymond Chandler, published in 1939, and *The Maltese Falcon* by Dashiell Hammett, published in 1930, both by Alfred A. Knopf. Both originally appeared as serialisations in *Black Mask*, also a Knopf publication.

'God Shall Wipe All Tears Away' is a gospel song recorded by Mahalia Jackson in 1935, and sung before that by Clara Butt.

'John the Revelator' is a gospel song recorded by 'Blind' Willie Johnson in 1930.

The poem quoted by Patricia: the original (English) title is 'No one puts their children in a boat unless the water is safer than the land' by Warsan Shire, first published in 2010.

I would like to thank my editors Laura Coulman-Rich and Jon Appleton, Kate Ballard and Suzy Clarke, and all the wonderful team at Joffe Books.

Lastly, thanks once again to Adrienne Gould. And to Tim Boon, as ever.

THE JOFFE BOOKS STORY

We began in 2014 when Jasper agreed to publish his mum's much-rejected romance novel and it became a bestseller.

Since then we've grown into the largest independent publisher in the UK. We're extremely proud to publish some of the very best writers in the world, including Joy Ellis, Faith Martin, Caro Ramsay, Helen Forrester, Simon Brett and Robert Goddard. Everyone at Joffe Books loves reading and we never forget that it all begins with the magic of an author telling a story.

We are proud to publish talented first-time authors, as well as established writers whose books we love introducing to a new generation of readers.

We won Trade Publisher of the Year at the Independent Publishing Awards in 2023 and Best Publisher Award in 2024 at the People's Book Prize. We have been shortlisted for Independent Publisher of the Year at the British Book Awards for the last five years, and were shortlisted for the Diversity and Inclusivity Award at the 2022 Independent Publishing Awards. In 2023 we were shortlisted for Publisher of the Year at the RNA Industry Awards, and in 2024 we were shortlisted at the CWA Daggers for the Best Crime and Mystery Publisher.

We built this company with your help, and we love to hear from you, so please email us about absolutely anything bookish at feedback@joffebooks.com.

If you want to receive free books every Friday and hear about all our new releases, join our mailing list here: www.joffe-books.com/freebooks.

And when you tell your friends about us, just remember: it's pronounced Joffe as in coffee or toffee!

www.ingramcontent.com/pod-product-compliance
Lightning Source LLC
Chambersburg PA
CBHW011519170626
46810CB00010B/3419